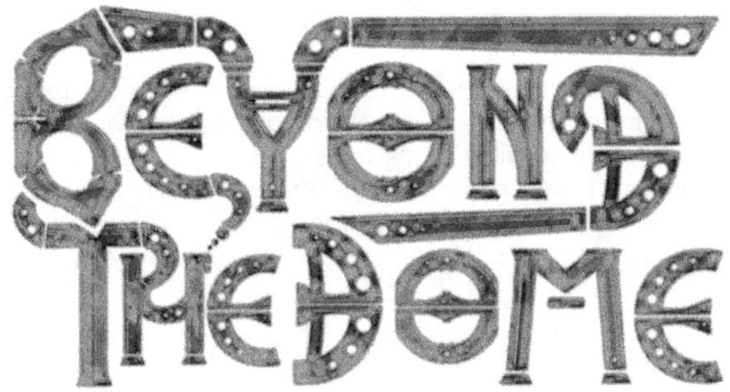

A COMEDY SCI-FI ADVENTURE SERIES

BY

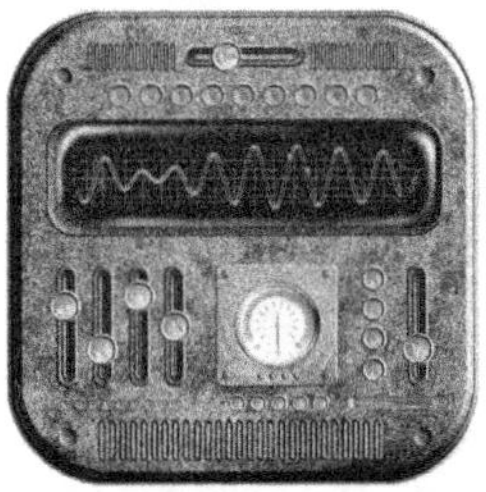

...I am almost tempted to press buttons and pull levers...

BOOK TWO

ISBN 978-1-7398855-2-6

Paper Version

BENEATH THE DOME BY SAM LUCAS © 2022

WWW.SAMLUCASBOOKS.COM
e-mail:samlucasbooks@btinternet.com

PUBLISHER - OSCAR PISCINE BOOKS

Following an explosion on board the *International Space Station*, Yuri and Dmitry leave their quarters and take their chances outside. Hovering 250 miles above the Earth like marionettes without a puppeteer, they consider their options. After a mere 12.2 seconds, they decide to return to the *Space Station* to investigate the full extent of the damage.

With only 30 minutes air supply left, Yuri and Dmitry use their jetpacks to manoeuvre closer to the *Space Station*, which is now moving violently and tugging at the support cables attached to the Dome...

ACT I, SCENE I

Our scene starts with Dmitry and Yuri in their space suits floating outside of the *International Space Station*. A light blue glow emanates from their jetpacks and they begin to move closer to evaluate the damage caused by the explosion. As they draw near, gas is seen venting from a hole in the port side and a fire is burning in the English astronauts quarters on the starboard side. The *Space Station* is rocking violently and the cables attached to the Dome are starting to lose their cohesion. Dmitry and Yuri enter the *Station* through a big hole where part of the structure is missing. Inside, they begin to investigate.

DMITRY

Quickly Yuri, get inside and put out that fire! I will head to see where gas is venting from.

YURI

Okay, Dmitry...

    (Yuri grabs a fire extinguisher from a wall panel and makes his way along the corridor and puts out the fire on the starboard side. He notices an Air Docking Port and uses it.)

...Dmitry, can you hear me?

(Dmitry is breathing heavily)

DMITRY
Yes.

YURI
Fire is out!

DMITRY
Good. Quickly...

(Moaning can be heard.)

...Come back here and help me close off
this valve, it is stuck solid.

YURI
Okay, I am on my way.

(Yuri makes his way through the
Station where Dmitry is
struggling to turn a valve off
in the cargo bay.)

DMITRY
Good, you are here. Grab that spanner
and loosen that bolt and I will turn
valve.

YURI
Did you want me to use the 28mm ring
spanner or the monkey wrench?

                    DMITRY
I don't care, just make a choice. We
are running out of time.

                    YURI
I have also seen a socket set that
might do the job.

          (Yuri looks around for other
          options.)

                    DMITRY
What are you doing? I can't hold this
much longer it is burning my gloves,
choose something.

                    YURI
Okay, this will do...

          (Yuri picks up the ring
          spanner, then puts it back,
          picks up the wrench, drops it,
          then grabs the socket set.)

... Okay, here we go. Do it now
Dmitry!

          (They both turn together, a
          loud screech is heard and the
          venting gas stops. The Space
          Station stops shaking and slows
          to a gentle sway.)

                    DMITRY
We did it Yuri. We are safe for a
minute...

> (Dmitry looks around the room
> and then at his air supply.)

...I only have 19 minutes air left.
How long do you have?

                    YURI
A little longer.

                    DMITRY
How much longer?

                    YURI
About 4 hours.

                    DMITRY
4 hours! How come you have nearly full
tank of oxygen?

                    YURI
Air Docking Port was still operational
on starboard side when we got on board,
so I used it. Did you not do the same
here?

> (Dmitry looks down at his burnt
> gloves and then looks back at
> Yuri.)

                    DMITRY
No, it is destroyed on this part of the
Station and I was a little busy. I
must go and use starboard docking port
now.

                    YURI
It is depleted. I took last of air.

                  DMITRY
Why did you do that? You have killed
me!

                    YURI
Don't worry. I pulled out coupling
cable and you can link to me. I will
give you some of my air. What did you
think Dmitry, that I would stab you in
back and enjoy remaining few hours of
my life watching your dead corpse float
around in this cargo bay like toy
balloon? Sorry to burst your bubble,
but we are in this mess together. We
are not dead yet, and if we put our
heads together we may get out of this
predicament and live to die another
day.

      (Yuri pulls out a cable from
      his backpack and attaches it to
      Dmitry to give him some air.)

                  DMITRY
Sorry Yuri, I guess I am a little
anxious and a drink would help take the
edge off of things.

                    YURI
A drink would be nice, but if you
remove helmet just now, you will not
live long enough to enjoy drink.
Better to focus on situation at hand.

                    DMITRY
You are right. We must stabilise
Station and get atmosphere back...

          (*Dmitry looks around the
          Station.*)

...Perhaps we could close off Russian
section from rest of ship, it looks
mainly undamaged. Each section was
built to be self-contained and should
support life for a couple of weeks.
That would be more than long enough for
a rescue mission. If we salvage what
we can from rest of ship, seal off our
sector and wait it out, we might make
it.

          (*The Space Station starts to
          sway again and a support cable
          breaks away from the Dome.
          Outside a window, they watch a
          large cable fall at great
          speed.*)

                    YURI
What is that big snake outside *Station*?
It looks like a Space Monster!

                    DMITRY
That is no Space Monster Yuri, it is
support cable. It must have broken
free from Dome. This is not good Yuri,
weight of cable and speed it is
falling, could be disastrous. You
better hold on to something.

*(Yuri looks around for
something to cling to and grabs
Dmitry.)*

DMITRY
Not me. Grab something solid. Look
over there, let's get inside that
storage area and wrap ourselves up in
net. It is strong and will cushion
jolt.

YURI
Okay, what will we do with boxes?

DMITRY
Throw some of them into corridor to
make room, and then close hatch.
Quickly Yuri...

*(Dmitry and Yuri throw boxes,
bags, metal rods and computer
parts out into the corridor.
Outside the window, the support
cable and part of the Dome
attachment go sailing by.)*

...That will do. Strap yourself in
Yuri and hold on.

*(The Space Station starts to
rock violently and then a loud
metallic scraping sound is
heard, and then - silence...)*

YURI
Dmitry, it's over?

                    DMITRY
I... I don't think so.

          (Boom... A huge piece of metal
          structure snaps away and sparks
          shower the area. A metal
          groaning noise begins shortly
          afterwards followed by a long
          scraping sound. The Space
          Station vibrates violently and
          Yuri and Dmitry begin bouncing
          around in the cargo net as the
          Station rocks back and forth.)

                    YURI
I hope this is over soon?

          (A knocking sound is heard and
          then dissipates into the
          distance.)

                    DMITRY
I think it's stopped. But we have
bigger problem.

                    YURI
What is that?

                    DMITRY
It is only matter of time before
remaining four cables lose their
cohesion with Dome...

          (Dmitry and Yuri pull
          themselves free of the cargo
          net.)

...if we are lucky we have 3 days at
most. Now one cable has gone, the
others will follow; just like dominoes
in row.

                    YURI
Maybe, if we are lucky, we can get
rescued before then?

                    DMITRY
Maybe. Let's hurry Yuri, one thing at
a time. Keep to original plan and seal
off ship. Grab everything you think we
might need, and I will see you back at
quarters. I don't think we have time
to see what caused explosion.

                    YURI
Okay, Dmitry.

          (Yuri walks out into the
          corridor and moves out of
          sight. Dmitry looks around the
          cargo bay for items to take and
          grabs a bar from the floor and
          pokes open a box marked
          'WHISKY'. Inside he discovers
          four bottles of liquid gold
          with the label -
          'GLENCRAOBHMARBH'. He places a
          couple of bottles in his space
          suit and leaves.)

Scene fades.

ACT 1, SCENE 2

Outside the Space Station, a debris field of metal shards, boxes and packets of powdered egg swirl around a large hole where part of the Station used to be. A grey misty vapour lingers around the hole and wafts intermittently inside the corridor of the *Space Station* and caresses the hatch to the Russian sector. Inside, Dmitry turns the dial on a radio and tries to contact Mission Control. Yuri enters holding a mangled device - part of a bomb. He throws it in front of Dmitry and then removes his helmet and gloves. The Russian section of the ship is now sealed off and the air pressure and gravity have returned to normal.

                    YURI
I wouldn't do that if I were you,
Dmitry.

          (*Dmitry looks down at the
          device and stops twiddling the
          radio dial.*)

                    DMITRY
Is that what I think it is?

                    YURI
Yes, and there are 3 more just like it.

DMITRY
Are they still active?

*(Dmitry picks up the device and
studies it.)*

YURI
No, they have been deactivated.

DMITRY
Deactivated? How is that possible?

YURI
Boris, I mean Doris, did not only chew
her way through our console, she was
particularly attracted to orange wire
casing on bomb. I believe this is wire
for remote detonation.

*(Dmitry gets to his feet and
looks at Yuri.)*

DMITRY
Yuri, do you know what this means?
That mouse of yours has saved us. If
those other devices had gone up we
would be dead now...

*(Dmitry paces the room, then
looks at Yuri.)*

...but it also means sabotage!

*(Yuri throws his gloves onto
the table and takes a seat. He
picks up his little tartan*

*bear, takes out a cigarette and
lights it.)*

YURI
But by whom, those devices must have
been here long before our tour
started...

*(Yuri takes a long drag from
his cigarette.)*

...something is not right Dmitry, it is
not clear to me yet, but I will figure
it out.

DMITRY
Yuri, what do you mean you will figure
it out? Up until yesterday you thought
we had actually gone to moon and an
apogee was a type of Indian warrior.
Today you are super sleuth like 19th
Century detective with big pipe and
deerstalker hat.

*(Yuri takes another satisfying
puff of his cigarette and blows
it at Dmitry.)*

YURI
I might be ill informed, but I am not
stupid. What you might consider
important and useful, I might consider
redundant and pointless. I like to fly
by seat of pants, where as you like old
ladies bloomers. You did not think
that we might still be in danger, you

instantly tried to contact *Mission Control* - that is your textbook brain working, I, on the other hand, smelt fish in coat pocket. If we are going to survive this ordeal, we must think before we act and know who is Shark and who is Dolphin.

DMITRY

Your fishy metaphors are lost on me, what do you mean?

YURI

I mean, *Mission Control* must have known about those explosive devices. I bet you, right now they are telling world about our demise. They will be celebrating safe return of English astronauts and promoting big story of *Space Station* malfunction and huge explosion. The English will be heroes and the Russian's will be villains.

    (Dmitry starts pulling some jackets out of a cupboard and grabs a small T.V.)

DMITRY

I have an idea Yuri. Clear that side. Let's see what they are saying about us.

    (Yuri clears the side and takes the T.V. from Dmitry and plugs it in.)

YURI
What will we do for aerial?

(Dmitry picks up a jacket he
threw out of the cupboard,
removes a coat hanger and hands
it to Yuri.)

DMITRY
Here, use this coat hanger...

(Dmitry pulls a cable from a
wall panel and passes it to
Yuri.)

...Bare wire on this cable and wrap
around coat hanger and plug other end
into back of T.V. Here is remote
control.

(Yuri plugs in the cable and
passes the coat hanger for
Dmitry to hold.)

...Turn it on Yuri.

YURI
Okay, let's try the News Station...

(The picture comes on but it is
fuzzy.)

...Try holding hanger higher.

DMITRY
What! Are you crazy?   We are 250

miles above the earth and you want me to hold hanger higher. I will attach it to metal frame, this connects all of *Space Station* together.

                    YURI
Don't move that's it!

                    DMITRY
I don't have it anymore. Turn it up. What are they saying?

          (Dmitry and Yuri move back from the T.V. to see the picture and Yuri turns up the sound.)

                    YURI
Hey look, it's us!

          (Pictures of Yuri and Dmitry are shown in their cosmonaut suits and then a lady newscaster starts to speak. They listen to the T.V.)

                    NEWS REPORTER
...Once again, today's headlines. Three astronauts and two Russian cosmonauts are believed dead after an explosion on board the *International Space Station* early this morning. The two Russian cosmonauts, Yuri Chekov and Dmitry Usakov, were at the start of their 3 month tour and had only been on board for a few days when the incident occurred. Reports are sketchy at the

moment, but it is believed they died instantly after a fire broke out in their quarters. The Russian Prime Minister, Mikhail Kantcoughsky, said the two cosmonauts were Russia's finest and would be honoured next Thursday at a special banquet ceremony at the Four Seasons hotel. (New News Story) A Russian 14 year old boy has become the first person in the world to eat 79 savoury beef crepes at the...

(T.V. is muted)

DMITRY

Those lousy, stinking, faceless, pen pushing, snuff sniffers. They have sold us down the Mezen river. Can you believe that halfwit Kantcoughsky, holding a banquet in our honour, the nerve. Any excuse to have a meal; I knew him as a boy you know - big fat chubby little fellow, always eating chocolate and stuffing toilet paper down his pants. At weekends he would go to jumble sale and sell paper as crepe gift wrap. What a snake. He also had the most annoying habit in classroom of bringing up phlegm and swallowing it back down. It was always followed by a silent cough and an involuntary wheeze. He was an overstuffed greasy olive then, now he is bloated stale fish with glasses. I can't believe he has the audacity to promote benefits of food stamps and health supplements to Russian

population, while he eats like hog.
What a scumbag. I would like to be at
that banquet next Thursday, I would
tell him a thing or two.

                    YURI
I get the feeling you don't like our
Prime Minister, but what do you think
this means, Dmitry? The News reporter
said we were all dead, even the
English.

                    DMITRY
I am not sure, but I don't think they
were expecting English astronauts to
survive. They must have found escape
pod by now. They must be deciding what
to do about them. If they have landed
in Pacific ocean, perhaps they will
drown. We will have to wait and see.
At moment they think we are dead and
Space Station is in bits; that will buy
us a little time, but we must come up
with plan.

                    YURI
Let me pour you drink Dmitry, I have a
little vodka in one of my tennis shoes
in that locker behind you.

                    DMITRY
Why do you have tennis shoes?

                    YURI
To carry my vodka, where else would I
keep it?

(Dmitry jumps out of his seat.)

                    DMITRY
Yuri, turn up T.V., Quickly!

*(The same lady Newscaster is
still reporting.)*

                  NEWS REPORTER
...In a remarkable turn of events, the
two English astronauts on board the
International Space Station, who were
first thought to have died in an
explosion earlier this morning, have in
fact survived. Astronauts George
London and Albert Wells managed to get
to the escape pod before the blast
engulfed the *Station*. We go live now
to the H.M.S Victorious, who is
currently in the middle of the Pacific
ocean...

                    DMITRY
Quick Yuri, grab video camera and
record T.V. screen...

     *(Yuri rummages through a metal
     box and takes out a video
     camera and switches it on.)*

...Yuri hurry, they are lowering escape
pod by helicopter onto deck.

                     YURI
I nearly have it, let me put in new
storage card and plug it in.

                    DMITRY
The pod is on deck, I can see movement,
the door is opening - hurry.

                    YURI
There, it is on. I will mount it on
tripod for good stability. Okay

                    DMITRY
It is on, yes?

                    YURI
Yes!

          (Yuri takes his seat and grabs
          a cigarette from his little
          tartan friend. Dmitry looks
          for some glasses to pour out
          some vodka for both of them.
          He pours a good shot in both
          glasses, hands one to Yuri and
          also sits down. They look at
          the T.V. and an English
          reporter is standing on the
          deck of the ship outside the
          pod - the hatch opens on the
          pod and out walk George London
          and Albert Wells. The
          helicopter flies away.)

              T.V. REPORTER
...Here, on board the H.M.S Victorious,
the excitement can barely be contained.
After only a few hours mourning the
loss of our two brave astronauts,
George London and Albert Wells, they

are back on Earth safe and sound...

                    DMITRY
Look at that scum, smiling away as if
they have been on vacation to Hawaii.
Look at that stupid flag waving in
background - rule Britannia my foot.
They would not cheer if they knew they
had abandoned us to die, they would
throw stones and call them sour names.
Britain is a great nation, but even a
wolf will chew its own foot off to get
out of trap. I can't wait to hear what
they have to say.

                    YURI
Dmitry, take a drink and chill out.
Let me listen.

          (Dmitry takes a drink and
          refills his glass and they
          return to the T.V. The camera
          zooms in close and George
          London begins to talk.)

               GEORGE LONDON
...We are glad to be back home and to
have survived a terrible ordeal on
board the *Space Station*. Our thoughts
now lie with our Russian and American
colleagues who tragically died suddenly
from an uncontrollable fire...

          (George London is interrupted
          by a naval officer and the two
          astronauts are led away and it

*cuts back to the studio. Yuri
mutes the sound on the T.V. and
turns off his video recorder.)*

DMITRY

I think our goose is cooked Yuri, if we
contact *Mission Control*, I believe they
will launch missile and destroy us.
They do not want us alive. It is clear
to me now. No *Space Station*, no
pictures - no flat earth. It is as
simple as that. Everyone can go about
their business thinking world is ball.
It would take years to build another
Space Station, and in present economic
climate, no one will be rushing to
invest in space exploration.

*(Yuri is busy reviewing the
video footage and shouts out.)*

YURI

*Dmitry! Dmitry! Come see.
Look!*

*(Yuri passes the video camera
to Dmitry.)*

DMITRY

What is it, I have seen it.

YURI

Look close behind George and Albert on
the deck.

(Dmitry looks closely at the

screen.)

DMITRY
I don't believe it, that is your mouse
with five little ones trailing behind
her. They have jumped from pod and
onto deck. They have now disappeared
down crack.

YURI
I am so happy, Doris and her babies are
safe.

DMITRY
Well as long as your mouse is safe,
that is the main thing. It would have
been a shame if we had made it back and
your mouse was left up here.

   *(Dmitry passes Yuri back the
   camera. Yuri is still
   smiling.)*

YURI
Yes, that would have been awful. You
are being sarcastic - that mouse has
saved us so far, she is Russian hero.

DMITRY
Russian hero, you have an exaggerated
opinion of that mouse. It doesn't even
have a brain, it saw some wire and
chewed it, that's what mice do, they
chew things. I only hope on H.M.S
Victorious they have insulated cables
or they will soon have fire.

                    YURI
The trouble with you Dmitry is that you
can't handle being saved by a mouse.

                    DMITRY
We are not safe yet, that mouse of
yours may have bought us a little time,
but we are only going to fall to our
deaths or suffocate in a few days time.

        *(Yuri looks saddened by
        Dmitry's words.)*

                    YURI
Perhaps we should get a little sleep.
Things will seem better after we have
rested for a while, and when we wake
up, I will cook us some food.

                    DMITRY
Yuri, that is a good idea. I am tired,
it has been a hectic day.

Scene fades.

ACT I. SCENE 3

Dmitry is fast asleep in his chair and is clinging to a half full vodka bottle. He is snoring and has the occasional hiccup between each grunt. Yuri has tidied up the quarters and everything looks shipshape. On the side, there are some neatly sliced vegetables and a vacuum packed leg of lamb. His gas burner is firmly planted on the table and a pan of water is coming to the boil. A coffee machine is now on the corner unit and is churning out an espresso.

                    YURI
Dmitry, wake up!

          *(Dmitry continues to sleep and
          the coffee machine adds a fine
          drone to his grunting.)*

Dmitry, wake up. There is fresh coffee.

                    DMITRY
...I told you, just another half hour. Go and see if eggs are ready, the blacksmith has made me some new shoes with gold thread and beads of Jade with Abalone inlay...

                    YURI
Dmitry, wake up!

                    DMITRY
What, where I am. This is not my
apartment, and who are you, you are not
Olga.

                    YURI
I am Yuri.

                    DMITRY
Yuri? Yuri... What has happened?

                    YURI
You have drunk half a bottle of vodka
and a full bottle of whisky, that's
what's happened.

                    DMITRY
Oh, my head. Oh, now I remember. We
are still here, how long did I sleep?

                    YURI
Six hours.

        (*Dmitry rubs his face and eyes.
        He looks very ill.*

                    DMITRY
Six hours! Why did you let me sleep so
long?

                    YURI
I have been trying to wake you for the
last two hours, but you have continued
to snore like pig. There is a coffee
for you. Drink it.

                    DMITRY
Did the maid come while I was asleep?
Everywhere looks great...

        (Dmitry takes a drink of
        coffee.)

...It is a good thing everywhere is
tidy, imagine the embarrassment for our
families when this thing crashes back
to Earth and they find what is left of
our quarters in a mess - oh, the shame.

                    YURI
Cleaning makes me think...

        (Yuri adds the vegetables and
        lamb to the pan and throws in a
        few spices.)

...besides, I needed a distraction from
the frogs chorus.

                    DMITRY
What frogs chorus, oh, did I snore?

                    YURI
Like fat woman with gas mask on.

                    DMITRY
Sorry, but I snore when I drink.
Anymore coffee?

                    YURI
Yes, just put your cup underneath
machine and press button.

*(Dmitry places his cup
underneath the coffee machine
and Yuri stirs his stew.)*

DMITRY
I don't suppose you came up with plan
while I slept?

YURI
Well, actually I did, but I could not
wake you, so I thought I would make
stew. A good stew will set us up for a
while and a full belly is a happy
belly...

*(Yuri takes out a cigarette and
lights it.)*

...I will tell you plan, if you are up
to it.

DMITRY
Don't worry about me, I am at my best
when I am hung over, it filters out all
the other rubbish.

YURI
Well, I was thinking... We can't call
Mission Control, but what if we send a
message to some radio 'HAM' via an
orbiting satellite and get them to tell
the world we are alive.

*(Dmitry picks up another coffee
and takes his seat again.)*

DMITRY

This is your plan? It sounds like a
good plan. Well at least it would be
if we did not know truth about planet.

YURI

What truth?

DMITRY

I don't suppose you have any relatives
with dementia in your family?

(Dmitry takes a sip of coffee
and Yuri tastes his stew.)

YURI

Dementia? What has that got to do with
anything?

DMITRY

Well, first of all, there are no
orbits, and secondly, there are no
satellites. If the fact the first two
parts of your idea were not bad enough,
you expect a perfect stranger to accept
on faith that you are Yuri Chekov on
board the now blown up *International
Space Station*. This is your plan?

YURI

What do you mean, no satellites? How
do we get Radio, T.V. and
Telecommunications? What about
Spudnik? Russia was first to launch
satellite in 1957. At last count there
were over a thousand satellites in

space.

>   (*Yuri turns away from his stew
>   and looks at Dmitry.*)

DMITRY
Yuri, look out window. Tell me how
many satellites you see?

>   (*Yuri looks out the window*)

YURI
None. There are none...

>   (*Yuri turns back and looks at
>   Dmitry and mutters.*)

...First the moon, Armsweak and
Oldsong, now Spudnik.

>   (*Yuri picks up his little
>   tartan friend, cuddles him,
>   then takes a cigarette.*)

...Dmitry, is everything lie? What was
Spudnik for?

DMITRY
Yuri, sit down. What I am about to
tell you, not many people know, but
seeing as we are going to be dead in a
few days, what does it matter. It will
help pass time while we wait for your
fine stew.

>   (*Yuri sits down and takes a*

*drag from his cigarette and
Dmitry takes his seat and
places his coffee on the side
and then looks at Yuri.)*

Back in the 1950's, we did not know
much about space travel and even less
about Dome. Ancient scrolls found in
Egyptian desert told us about structure
of Dome and its power source; we needed
a closer look, something that could
take pictures and send back real data.
In 1957, Soviet Union sent up Spudnik
in guise of satellite. The four
antennas attached to its sphere were
actually legs with special insulated
grips to cling to underside of Dome.
After 21 days studying and walking
inner surface of Dome it came back to
Earth. Except, there was a tiny little
problem.

                    YURI
What was that?

                    DMITRY
It crash landed in a farmer's field
near city of Irkutsk, eastern Siberia.
For next year it lay in mud amongst
some *Pink Fir Apple* potatoes the farmer
was experimenting with. Then one day,
while he was walking along drills, he
spotted a shiny object in dirt.

          *(Yuri looks on excitedly and
          asks with a high tone.)*

                    YURI
What was it Dmitry?

                  DMITRY
What do you mean? It was Spudnik!
Yuri, are you listening to story or
just staring at me with vacant look on
face until I finish monologue.

                    YURI
Sorry Dmitry, you mentioned potatoes,
and my stomach started to dream. Yes,
of course, it was Spudnik.

                  DMITRY
Later that day, when he returned home,
he took object to his wife, and that's
when the trouble began.

                    YURI
A woman and trouble are close cousin,
it always starts with a woman.

     (Dmitry looks around the
      quarters.)

Do you have anything to drink Yuri?

                    YURI
Yes, there is some bottled water in box
in corner, did you not get enough
coffee?

                  DMITRY
Yes, but do you not have anything

stronger, my throat is very dry, what
happened to the vodka?

    (Yuri passes Dmitry some
    bottled water.)

             YURI
I put it away for later. First finish
story and I will find you some brandy
to tide you over.

           DMITRY
Okay, Where was I?

            YURI
...and that's when the trouble began.

           DMITRY
Yes, that is right. The farmer gave
his wife the metal orb, which was not
much bigger than a basket ball, and
they studied it thinking it was a
silver serving bowl with lid. The four
legs had snapped off at base during its
return journey and now looked like the
items feet. They thought there might
be something inside it, maybe jewels or
coins, so they prised it open with a
meat cleaver. Inside they discovered a
camera and data punched cards and a
torn piece of paper with just the words
'AF4SB'...

            YURI
What does it mean Yuri?

                    DMITRY
...I still don't know...

          (Dmitry takes a drink from the
          bottled water and then
          continues.)

...As fortune would have it, the
farmer's wife was an amateur
photographer and had her own darkroom,
so she decided to develop film.
To her astonishment, the film contained
detailed images of the Dome and the
alien spaceship parked just on the
other side.

                    YURI
She must have got shock when she saw
photos of Dome and spaceship. What did
she do next?

                    DMITRY
She showed her husband and they decided
to take pictures to local newspaper.
The following day, paper is running
story about giant Dome and alien
spaceship. As you can imagine, it did
not take long for men in black coats to
appear at the farmer's house asking for
film. Two days later, there is
retraction printed in newspaper stating
that it was a hoax perpetrated by
farmer's wife.

                    YURI
So it wasn't true, she made it up?

DMITRY
Of course it was true...

      (Dmitry looks exasperated and
      rubs his face with both hands.)

...I don't think we are reading same
book Yuri, your book has lots of
colourful pictures about flowers and
Origami and is only ten pages long,
where as mine is encyclopaedia of life
with many volumes. If you concentrate
hard Yuri, you might actually learn
something.

YURI
Sorry Dmitry, but you are very
knowledgeable about this subject and
how devious people can be. I have not
dealt with many manipulators and
schemers. In my town, if you did not
like someone, you punched them in face.
There were no people with black coats,
most of the people in my neighbourhood
did not have a jacket, let alone
coat...

      (Yuri takes out a cigarette and
      lights it.)

...So, what happened next?

DMITRY
About a month later, the farmer has new
barn and combine harvester, and the
wife has a new pickup truck. What do
you make of that?

YURI

He had a successful harvest of Pink Fir
Apples?

DMITRY

No! They were paid to keep quiet about
what they had seen.

YURI

What about Newspaper, they would have
seen original photos?

DMITRY

Two months later, the editor is killed
in a terrible gas explosion at his
office and the Newspaper, along with
all the printing presses, are burnt to
ground.

YURI

That is quite a story Dmitry, it
certainly makes you think.   It has
given my brain cells a good workout and
my stomach a pleasing appetite.   I
think I will give the stew a stir.

     (Yuri gets up and stirs the pan
     of stew.)

So the farmer and his wife never said
anything about Dome or spaceship?

DMITRY

No, they couldn't, they never had a
chance.

                    YURI
What do you mean?

                    DMITRY
Shortly afterwards they were found dead
on their farm.

        (Yuri turns around from the
        stew and faces Dmitry.)

Dead. How did they die?

                    DMITRY
They were found cut up and mangled in
blades of combine harvester. Terrible
mess. It was reported as an accident
due to human error.

                    YURI
What a shame, they had only just built
new barn...

        (Yuri tastes his stew and adds
        some salt. He then turns
        around to face Dmitry waving a
        wooden spoon.)

...Farming is dangerous, I once had an
uncle who lost his finger whilst
chopping wood and died of bacterial
infection.

                    DMITRY
Don't you see Yuri, they were all
killed by covert government agency to
keep Dome a secret.

                    YURI
That is terrible, such a waste...

        (Yuri turns back to his stew
        and stirs it again.)

...to think of all those potatoes
rotting in ground and no one to harvest
them, it's unforgiveable. Just
imagine...

        (The lights go out and the
        power goes off. The gas burner
        is now the only source of
        light.)

...Dmitry, what has happened?

                    DMITRY
Listen...

        (They both stay quiet for a
        moment.)

...What is that hissing sound?

                    YURI
What hissing sound, the only thing I
can hear is gas burner.

                    DMITRY
That's it, that is noise. For a moment
I thought we were in trouble. We must
have blown a fuse and the breaker needs
resetting.

                    YURI
Is that outside the Russian section?

                    DMITRY
No, there is panel in corridor. I will
go and see, I'll just grab torch.

          *(Dmitry finds a torch and goes
          out into the corridor.)*

                    YURI
Hurry back, stew is almost ready.

Scene fades.

ACT 2. SCENE 1

After moving some boxes and containers in the corridor, Dmitry replaces a blown fuse and resets the circuit breaker. The lights spring back into life and the power is restored throughout the Russian sector of the *Space Station*. He replaces a panel and returns to Yuri. In their quarters, the lights are back on and the T.V. can be heard. Yuri has set the table and has laid out some bowls, spoons, napkins and glasses with a bottle of brandy. Two candles glow softly by the window and a puff of smoke rises into the air. Yuri is watching the T.V. and smoking a cigarette when Dmitry returns.

(Dmitry looks over to the T.V.)

DMITRY
Anything interesting?

YURI
I am waiting for News, but they keep showing pictures of storm IVAN. They say it is going to be a big storm, with winds over 150mph and that Moscow is going to be hit worst.

DMITRY
A big storm, just as well we are up here, we are quite safe from such things.

                    YURI
Take a seat Dmitry; stew is ready.

                   DMITRY
Good, I am quite hungry.

     (Yuri turns down the T.V.,
     dishes out the stew into two
     bowls and places them on the
     table. Dmitry takes his seat
     and so does Yuri.)

                   DMITRY
Mmm, this smells fantastic Yuri, and
looks even better.

                    YURI
Good. Oh, I almost forgot. We still
have some brioche to eat. It is in
container marked - 'Laser Cutter', in
locker behind you.

                   DMITRY
I will get it.

     (Dmitry reaches into the locker
     behind him and takes the bread
     from the container.)

                   DMITRY
I am not even going to ask where laser
cutter is, it does not matter
anymore...

     (He tastes the stew and makes a
     face of sheer delight, then

looks up at Yuri.)

...Yuri, I don't know why you went into *Space Programme*, you should have been chef. The food you have prepared so far on trip has been exceptional, and to be fair, has been highlight of space trek.

YURI
Thank you Dmitry, that means a lot. If I can keep our spirits up until end, I will do my best.

(Dmitry looks over to the T.V., where they are still showing pictures of a big storm heading towards Moscow. He points his spoon towards the T.V.)

DMITRY
Looks like that storm is going to be a corker Yuri, they are showing an incredible amount of high pressure over Russia...

(Dmitry gobbles down some stew.)

...and when that cold front hits that warm air and pressure drops - they are in for it. There will be a lot of roofs off houses tonight.

YURI
So, you are weather man now. It is

load of rubbish, they always hype up
these things, you have only just
finished telling me there are no
satellites in sky, so how can they
predict weather...

        (Yuri takes a piece of bread
        and mops up some stew and eats
        it.)

...it is brown deposit left in field by
bull. The main cause of roofs leaving
to find new home is cowboy builders.

                    DMITRY
Cowboy builders?

        (Dmitry stops eating and looks
        up at Yuri.)

                    YURI
Yes, cowboy builders. When I was boy,
I overheard conversation my mother was
having with my cousin Oleg. He was
telling her how his roof had parted
company with rest of house in 80mph
winds. Oleg couldn't understand why
house next door had no damage, and his
was ruined. It turns out, he had used
a different contractor and had paid a
lot less for house.

        (Dmitry breaks off some bread
        and eats it.)

43

DMITRY

You get what you pay for. Cheap is not always best.

YURI

That's what my father used to say every Friday night.

DMITRY

Why every Friday?

YURI

Oh, that was 'Steak Night'.

    *(Yuri adds some more stew to
    Dmitry's bowl and then to his
    own. Dmitry looks at Yuri
    perplexed.)*

DMITRY

I am sure there is link here somewhere Yuri, but could you help a dumb Russian cosmonaut out.

YURI

Oh, yes. Every Friday night was same in our house - 'Steak Night'. I would sit down to dinner and hope my father was in good mood. I would watch in suspense, as he tried to cut through steak with knife. After five minutes of unsuccessful strokes with knife, he would call through to kitchen, where my mother was still cooking steak for herself.

*(Yuri starts to impersonate his
father and mother.)*

FATHER
'Where did you buy this steak?'

MOTHER
'I got it from Rosko Reznik's the
butcher.'

FATHER
'How many times have I told you not to
get it from there. The meat is shipped
in from Czechoslovakia, and it is all
fat. Why did you not go to Myro
Myasnik's like I told you?'

MOTHER
'The meat is over twice the price and I
would have to walk another two miles to
get it.'

FATHER
'If you ask me, it is worth it - you
get what you pay for, and you could use
the exercise.'

YURI
At this point my mother would walk in
room and sit down at table with her
steak and start to stare at my father.

FATHER
'What? What are you looking at?'

                    MOTHER
'You think you are something, telling
me to buy a better steak when the army
didn't even give you a pension. Why
didn't you get your own steak instead
of lazing around apartment all day?
You are not the man I married, the man
I married was a fine handsome figure,
now you look like Santa Claus without
suit and beard. To think once you were
a General in Russian army, now you are
a disgusting pig!'

                    FATHER
'Be quiet woman before you get a
smack.'

                    MOTHER
'You are pathetic, and that slug on
your face you call a moustache looks
like a third eye brow.'

                    FATHER
'At least when I smile I show more than
one tooth!'

                    YURI
The evening would go on like this until
my father ran out of insults and
punched her in face.

        (Dmitry takes a swig of brandy
        and then looks at Yuri.)

                    DMITRY
Your father used to hit your mother?

YURI

Only on Friday, but she deserved it.

DMITRY

What do you mean? No one deserves to
get hit!

YURI

My mother does have an acid tongue and
she can be venomous if she wants.

DMITRY

I hope you do not hit your wife Yuri?

YURI

What, Ivanka? You are kidding, my wife
is hot head and has tropical temper,
but worst of all she is thinker! If I
was to ever hit her, I would wake up in
morning with knife in back. No, I am a
great believer in cool heads
prevailing. After an hour in dark
cupboard she would let me out and I
would apologise. Then she would give
me apple and blackberry crumble for my
pudding and then we would go upstairs
for dessert.

DMITRY

It seems you have an arrangement that
works for you...

        (Dmitry takes a last spoonful
        of stew and puts his spoon down
        in his bowl.)

...thanks Yuri, I am very full...

> *(Dmitry glances over at the silent T.V.)*

...Yuri, look! It's your wife Ivanka. Quick turn it up!

YURI

What?

> *(Yuri glances over at the T.V., grabs the remote and turns it up. Yuri's wife is delivering a speech to the press outside their family home.)*

IVANKA

...it has been confirmed today that my husband, Yuri Chekov and his cosmonaut comrade Dmitry Usakov are dead. Satellite images have shown us that the *International Space Station* has been destroyed and they would have had no chance of survival...

DMITRY

That's what you think.

IVANKA

...I would like to thank the Russian Space Programme for all their support since hearing the news of my husband's death...

                    YURI
But I am not dead, my love, I am here!

          (Ivanka continues her speech
          while Dmitry talks.)

                    DMITRY
Who is that beside your wife Yuri, he
has quite a close grip on her. Look!
He has squeezed her bottom and she
smiled a little. Look, he did it
again.

          (Yuri looks closer at the
          screen.)

                    YURI
That is my cousin Anatoly, he was at
house quite a lot before I came away.
He works for a big insurance company in
city, he persuaded me to double my life
insurance policy before I left for
tour.

                    DMITRY
And now he is very cosy with your
Ivanka. I must say your wife looks
heartbroken!

                    IVANKA
...I would also like to thank Yuri's
cousin Anatoly for being by my side at
this time of grief and sadness...

                    DMITRY
Look Yuri, she cannot even keep a

straight face, she is laughing now and
they think she is crying - what a
monster!

                    IVANKA
...I am sorry, I am going inside now...

          (*The picture cuts back to the
          News presenter, and Yuri turns
          down the sound.*)

                    YURI
What a slut. How could I have trusted
her. All those days I came home from
work and Anatoly was in house. I
thought he was just visiting and trying
to get business from rich relative.
Now it turns out he was snake, a viper
in bosom; and my wife, a cheap whore
with expensive hairdo. If I was not
going to die in a couple of days, I
would kill myself!

                    DMITRY
Don't take it so hard Yuri, these
things happen. You are away from home
a lot and your wife... Well, your wife
is a very attractive woman. Men take
advantage of these things, and she is
only human.

                    YURI
It is easy for you Dmitry, you have
very little faith in people and you
suspect the worst. You are fatalist
and drunk - that is your strength.

Your life is quite happy in gutter
smelling sewer stench, if things get
too bad, you have a drink - happy days!

                    DMITRY
It is good to see you hold me in such
high esteem. I would hate it if you
did not speak your mind and garnished
the truth with a little sprinkling of
diplomacy.

                    YURI
Sorry, Dmitry. I did not mean to be
unkind. I was quite happy to meet my
maker, knowing my wife would be secure
in her future, and that she wouldn't
have to worry about money. Now, all I
can see is that greasy little rat
Anatoly with his sticky little fingers
all over my wife...

        (Yuri takes the palm of his
        left hand and rubs it against
        the fist of his right.)

... and her smiling, while she is
telling world we are dead, what a
repulsive, vile sleaze bucket. I am
not sad anymore, I am angry and
relieved.

        (Yuri collects the dishes from
        the table and throws them in
        the waste bin.)

                    DMITRY
That is good Yuri. Let's watch T.V.
for a while, and maybe have a sleep.
There might be a good film on.

                    YURI
I am a bit tired. A film, yes.

        *(Yuri pours Dmitry another
        brandy and one for himself and
        they toast. The T.V. sound
        comes on, Yuri takes a seat and
        they both start to watch a
        movie.)*

Scene fades.

ACT 2. SCENE 2

It is Tuesday 14th October, 0400 hours. Dmitry and Yuri have been sleeping for several hours. The Space Station is still stable for the time being and the life support systems are functioning within normal parameters. Yuri and Dmitry are sleeping in their chairs, when suddenly Yuri is awoken by an alarm coming from the coffee machine. He walks over to the appliance and adds some water - the noise stops. Dmitry starts to move from his sleeping position and wakes up.

                    DMITRY
What time is it?

                    YURI
4am...

          (Yuri pours some coffee for the
          both of them and hands Dmitry a
          cup. Outside the window a huge
          cloud formation can been seen
          below.)

...Looks like that storm is getting worse.

                    DMITRY
Good.

53

                         YURI
Why is it good?

                        DMITRY
You heard your wife last night, she
told world, *Space Station* has been
destroyed.

          *(Yuri takes a cigarette from
          his little bear and lights it.)*

                         YURI
So, what does that matter?

                        DMITRY
Don't you see Yuri, it confirms what
you were saying, *Mission Control*
believe we are dead, but how do they
know? A normal response would be to
try and contact us in the hope there
were survivors. The radio is working
and our antenna is not broken, but we
have heard not one peep. It proves
they knew about bombs and that they
think we are space debris. The only
reason we are still alive is because of
storm - they just can't see us. Even
the 30" telescope at the Pulkovo
Observatory can't see through storm.
When maelstrom is over, so are we.

                         YURI
So, we don't have much longer. If this
thing doesn't detach itself from Dome
within next two days, we will survive
long enough to be blown apart by

missile.

                    DMITRY
You missed the third option Yuri.

                    YURI
What was that?

                    DMITRY
Life Support could give up at any
moment and we could suffocate.

          (Yuri takes a final look out
          the window and returns to his
          seat. He looks at the T.V. and
          sees something of interest and
          turns the sound up.)

                    YURI
Dmitry, look. It is Cammachmore
institute in Highlands of Scotland. I
went there when I was in my twenties.

                    DMITRY
Eh? What is it? What is that fool
saying? Turn up the volume.

          (A young female reporter is
          seen standing outside a big
          grey building with huge
          antennas. She is wearing a
          raincoat and holding a
          microphone.)

TV REPORTER

...We're outside the village of Tamich
in the Highlands of Scotland, where the
Cammachmore Weather Station is getting
ready to employ an experimental laser
to cut through the eye of storm IVAN,
which is currently tearing a path
towards Moscow. With me, is professor
Ronald MacTavish to explain the
process. Professor, would you care to
tells us what you do here and the
procedure you are about to carry out?

*(The camera moves to the left
and we see a grey-haired man in
his 60's wearing a green tweed
jacket and plaid trousers. He
is thin and dishevelled.)*

PROFESSOR MACTAVISH

... Certainly. At C.L.A.R.S.A.C.H.S,
THE CAMMACHMORE LAND ANTENNA FOR
REDUCING SEVERE ANOMALOUS CLIMATIC
HEMISPHERE STRESSES, we study and
measure atmospheric pressure throughout
the world. Over the years, we have
perfected a method of controlling the
weather by changing the pressure level
in any given region of the planet.
This will cause cold air to meet a warm
front and vice versa. This in turn
reverses the formation of storms such
as the one over Russia just now.

T.V. REPORTER

So, can you tell us how this method
works?

PROFESSOR MACTAVISH
Basically, we fire a great big laser
into the eye of the storm and it
dissipates over the next few hours.

T.V. REPORTER
When will you be firing this laser?

PROFESSOR MACTAVISH
About tea time tomorrow, Scottish time.

T.V. REPORTER
Thank you very much Professor. This is
Gillian Strachan reporting for Grampian
News...

(*Returns to* News Station. *Yuri
turns down the sound.*)

YURI
I can't believe it, imagine them
showing Cammachmore, I haven't seen
that place in over 20 years. Still
looks the same - cold and wet.

DMITRY
This is not good Yuri, we may have even
less time if they fire off that laser.

YURI
Don't worry Dmitry, it never worked 20
years ago, I don't suppose it'll work
now.

                    DMITRY
What do you mean?

                    YURI
Institute was ruse perpetrated by my
aunt to get government grants. Most of
money went to church hall refurbishment
and new buildings like school. They
also built a supermarket, a cinema and
a swimming pool.

                    DMITRY
What are you saying Yuri?

        (*Yuri gets up and grabs the
        coffee pot, pours Dmitry some
        more coffee and tops up his own
        cup. He then lights a
        cigarette and sits down.*)

                    YURI
Many applications were made to local
council for improvements to facilities,
all were denied. Local community were
in despair. Then, an opportunity
arose, my aunt, who had recently moved
from Russia to Cammachmore, became a
member on town council. For most of
her adult life she had been part of
Russian *Space Programme* from as early
back as the 1950's and was very well
qualified in quantum physics and
meteorology. On council, she became
aware of little loop hole in grant
applications for scientific study. To
help local community get school and

swimming pool, she put in application
for *Weather Station*, and it was
approved. The rest is, as you would
say, history. They have been siphoning
off funds for local community ever
since. So this Wednesday when the
CLARSACHS institute fire that laser, it
will be good display of fireworks.

                    DMITRY
But what about storm?

                    YURI
Dmitry, storms dissipate anyway, and
the next day is blue sky - no laser
required!

                    DMITRY
I hope you are right. The longer we
have grey skies over Moscow the
better...

        (Dmitry drinks his coffee and
        then places the cup on the
        table.)

...just out of curiosity, why did your
aunt move to this Cammachmore place?

                    YURI
Her husband was from there. After they
retired from work in Moscow, they
decided to go to family home near
Tamich, in Scotland. It was a nice big
manor house with quite a sizable
estate. They had never made much use

of it in their working years, except an occasional holiday, so they decided to retire there and live out remaining days.

                    DMITRY
How did you come to visit?

                    YURI
My mother and father were thinking about a divorce and mother suggested that I go stay with my aunt Annuska for a while. So I was bundled off to Cammachmore in Scotland for three months.

                    DMITRY
So this is how you learnt about *Weather Station?*

                    YURI
Yes, but it wasn't by design.

                    DMITRY
What do you mean?

                    YURI
My aunt Annuska was a lot older than my mother and was suffering the late stages of Alzheimer's and would talk a lot when we were in fields collecting jars of daylight.

                    DMITRY
Jars of daylight?

YURI

My aunt had this notion that if you collected last rays of sunlight in jam jar, it would give off eternal illumination. She would hurry home after collection and place jars in basement locker.

(Dmitry gets up and stretches, yawns, then returns to his seat. Yuri takes out another cigarette.)

DMITRY

I take it she didn't have any luck with that?

YURI

No, she had been doing it for years. She started collecting darkness from night with no moon, but darkness always went away when she turned on basement light. It was sad to see, but she could be quite talkative and lucid at times.

DMITRY

What about her husband, how did he deal with it?

YURI

Sandy? He was worse than her. He became obsessed with carpet fibres and their attraction to dust particles. He also had jam jars in locker full of

dust from neighbours houses. On a
sheet of plywood in garage he had
collected over 2,000 fibres from
different carpets - he was banned from
all the local floor specialist shops.
I can see him now: tartan trousers,
herringbone cap, geometric patterned
jumpers and golf shoes.

                    DMITRY
Did he like golf? There are quite a
lot of good golf courses in Scotland.

                    YURI
No, he couldn't play, but he thought
golf club was a good place to get dust
samples from customer shoes.

                    DMITRY
He sounds like a real character. I
take it they are both dead?

                    YURI
Yes, my aunt Annuska died only a month
after my visit, but Sandy lived another
year then died in plane crash.

                    DMITRY
A plane crash?

                    YURI
Yes, after my aunt died he applied for
his pilot's licence. After passing
test, he bought himself a Cessna 172
Skyhawk, and after only one day flying

solo, he crashed into tree trying to
land on golf course.

                    DMITRY
Shame. How old was he?

                    YURI
He was 92. A good age. I think I have
a picture here somewhere.

          (Yuri rummages around in a
          case and pulls out a black book
          with gold lettering. The cover
          reads, 'TRADITIONAL RUSSIAN
          RECIPES'. From inside, he
          removes a picture of his aunt
          Annuska and his uncle Sandy
          standing in front of a 1958
          ZIL-111 automobile. He hands
          the picture to Dmitry.)

                    DMITRY
They look very happy, and that is a
very nice car they have.

                    YURI
It was brand new at time, they only had
car, I believe, for one day when photo
was taken.

          (Dmitry turns the photo over
          and reads the back.)

                    DMITRY
...'Annuska Fedorov and Sandy Brown.
1958, ZIL-111 automobile. 1 Month

before we got married'...

   *(On the bottom of the card it
   reads.)*

'...Thanks Spudnik!   AF4SB...

   *(Yuri looks at Dmitry and
   Dmitry begins muttering the
   same words over and over -
   'AF4SB'.)*

                    YURI
AF4SB. Wasn't that that code you could
never break Dmitry. Why are you
muttering it now?

                   DMITRY
Yuri! AF4SB. They were in love, they
had not yet got married and were in
glorious salad days of relationship.
They sent a message of love and hope to
space.

                    YURI
Who?

                   DMITRY
Who? Your aunt and uncle that's who.
AF - Annuska Fedorov, 4, meaning FOR,
SB - Sandy Brown.

                    YURI
Dmitry, you have cracked code after all
these years and I have had answer in
recipe book for the last twenty. I

can't believe it, the answer was under your nose all this time.

DMITRY
I tried every possible algorithm to crack code and never once thought it was somebody's initials. After all these years Yuri, I really thought it was secret code.

YURI
Let's have a drink to my aunt and uncle.

(Yuri pours out some brandy and they toast to his aunt and uncle.)

DMITRY
...to Annuska and Sandy. Na Zdorovie!

Scene fades.

ACT 2. SCENE 3

Dmitry and Yuri slept for a little while then had breakfast. They have spent the last hour tidying up their quarters and getting rid of all the rubbish, emptying ash trays, washing plates and cleaning down the sides. They have also washed their bodies and look cleanly shaved. They are now wearing the standard grey issue space boiler suit, which exhibits a double yellow stripe on the trouser outside left leg. New candles have been placed at the window and are emitting a soft yellow glow and enhance the lighting in the room. Through the window, the Earth below is being hammered by storm Ivan and a major cyclone can be seen over Russia. The T.V. is showing waves crashing against a shore and windy weather; the volume is turned down. A *scrabble* board is on the table and Yuri is about to pick his first seven letters. Dmitry has already got his letters and is rearranging them on his rack.

> *(Dmitry starts to lay his*
> *letters on the board, and he*
> *starts to smile.)*

DMITRY
J. U. M. B. U. C. K - 'Jumbuck', that is double word score, plus 50 points for seven letters, that is - 8, 16, 17, 20, 23, 24, 27, 32 x 2 = 64 + 50 = 114

points.   Your turn.   Beat that if you
can!

    (Yuri has finished picking his
    letters and is rearranging
    them.)

            YURI
Jumbuck?   What is that, you made it up?

          DMITRY
It is Australian sheep, immortalised in
song 'Waltzing Matilda'.

           YURI
Okay, Just my luck, rotten letters -
Ah, J.A.M - 'Jam', that is 8,9,12 - 12
points.   I think I am off to a bad
start...

    (Yuri leans forward to take
    more letters from the bag and
    accidentally touches the remote
    control and changes the channel
    on the T.V. and deactivates the
    'Mute' button. A Press
    conference can be seen and two
    men join a another on the
    stage.)

...Sorry Dmitry, I will turn it off.
Dmitry look! Look who it is!

    (Dmitry looks at the T.V. and
    sees George London and Albert
    Wells take a seat at what

*appears to be a Press
conference.)*

DMITRY
It is those English rats who have left
us to die. I wonder what fantastical
flights of fancy they will delight and
captivate the Press with. This should
be interesting Yuri, turn it up so we
can hear their decorative lies.

*(Yuri turns up the T.V., a man
dressed smartly with a tie
starts to speak.)*

SPOKESMAN
... George London and Albert Wells have
willingly consented to this Press
conference to answer any questions you
may have about the recent tragedy on
board the I.S.S. Please keep your
questions short and to the point, thank
you...

*(The man walks off stage, and
we see George London and Albert
wells seated at a table with a
microphone in front of them.)*

MALE REPORTER
Do you know how the fire started on
board the I.S.S?

GEORGE LONDON
Yes, it started in the Russian section
of the *Space Station* and quickly swept

through each sector like a fireball.
The Russians were cooking with a gas
stove and I believe it exploded.
Instead of eating the food supplied to
them by the Space Programme, they chose
to eat food they took with them.

                ANOTHER MALE REPORTER
You say the Russians were cooking with
a gas stove? Isn't that dangerous?

                GEORGE LONDON
Incredibly. But they did not want to
eat the ration packs provided.

                WOMAN REPORTER
Can you tell us what's in those packs?

                GEORGE LONDON
Erm, let me think - Powdered egg, bacon
in a tube... dried soya milk, oat
cakes, ...orange dust flakes, erm,
milled lentils, desiccated rhubarb,
...dehydrated pancakes, cured chocolate
and some vitamin pills and other
supplements.

                YURI
I don't know about you Dmitry, but he
is making me hungry.

                DMITRY
Yes, milled lentils always entice me to
eat, even when I am full.

YURI
*It was the 'Orange Dust Flakes'
that pricked my ears up!*

(They both laugh.)

WOMAN REPORTER
So, you are sure the Russians started
the fire that led to the destruction of
the *Space Station*?

GEORGE LONDON
Pretty sure. They had caused a fire
the day before and burnt a console in
their quarters and took out a few
circuit boards on the computer's
mainframe. I had also seen them
smoking on several occasions.

DMITRY
Those dirty little scumbags, sitting
there all pious and innocent, I can't
take it!

GEORGE LONDON
Dmitry Usakov, the Russian leader for
their sector, was seen drinking vodka
many times and was often drunk.

FEMALE REPORTER
Those are serious allegations you are
making, are these not just fabricated
stories you are telling us to hide your
guilt in these matters?

GEORGE LONDON

No, not at all. If you check with
Russian Mission Control I am sure they
will verify these facts for you.

ANOTHER REPORTER

I believe, according to official
documentation and schematics, that
there are 7 seats available in the
I.S.S's escape pod. Why did you not
wait for the other three colleagues on
board the *Station* before you ejected?

ALBERT WELLS

I would like to answer this. We got to
the escape pod with flames travelling
down the corridor behind us, as George
said, it was sweeping through each
section like a fireball - the Russian
sector was the first to go, meaning it
must have started there. I turned
around and saw Hank Johnson, the
American astronaut, running towards us
when he got engulfed in the fire. When
he reappeared a few seconds later, half
of his upper body was missing. We kept
the pod door open for as long as we
could; George burnt his hand badly
closing it. When another explosion
occurred we pulled the lever and left.
Seconds later the *Space Station*
exploded. We are lucky to be alive, we
weren't the one's who brought a mouse
on board and started fires. The
Russians caused this fire, plain and
simple.

ANOTHER REPORTER
A mouse you say?

ALBERT WELLS
Yes, looked like a little Panda. I saw
it twice. Yuri Chekov was always
creeping about at 4am looking for it -
'Boris, Boris where are you?' I believe
it was chewing on vital wiring from the
mainframe computer, and also
contributed towards the fire.

SAME REPORTER
Why did you not report this to your
commanding officer at Mission Control?

ALBERT WELLS
George and I had talked over the Dmitry
and Yuri situation that morning, and
decided to make a full report to
Mission Control, and that's what we did
- it's in the log. I guess we were just
too late.

*(The man with the tie walks
back on the stage looking a
little distraught and is
perspiring profusely.)*

SPOKESMAN
Thank you all very much for coming
today, I think Mr. London and Mr. Wells
have been more than free with their
responses to your questions, all
further questioning will be postponed
until after the board of inquiry.

*(George London and Albert Wells
are hurried off the stage.)*

DMITRY
They sure make us look bad Yuri, I am a
drunkard and you are a pyromaniac with
a mouse. Turn the T.V. down Yuri.
They are making us out to be
irresponsible fools, it couldn't be
worse!

*(Yuri turns down the T.V.
volume.)*

YURI
You are right, it couldn't be worse
Dmitry, all I have are vowels.

DMITRY
What do you mean vowels? Our
reputation has been ruined and you are
worrying about stupid game of *Scrabble?*

YURI
It is alright for you, you are over a
hundred points in lead and all I have
are six vowels and one consonant, I am
finished!

*(Yuri lights a cigarette and
sits back in his chair. Dmitry
stares at him bewildered.)*

DMITRY
I can't believe you are not bothered by
what English have just said - they have

lied to world and we are laughing
stock!

                    YURI
What would you like me to say Yuri, I
cannot do anything about a Press
conference 250 miles away when I am
stuck in broken *Space Station* with no
hope of escape. If you want something
to worry about, you should be focusing
on why they left Press conference
halfway through and hurried off stage.

                    DMITRY
Why would I worry about that?

                    YURI
Obviously, someone has pointed
telescope in sky and has seen that
Space Station is not in little pieces.
If this news gets out, English cover
story is, how you say - UP IN SMOKE.
It is now only matter of time before
storm clears and they launch missile -
POOF!

          *(Yuri gets up and takes a
          bottle of vodka from a locker
          and pours each of them a tall
          drink, then sits back down.)*

                    DMITRY
I see. There must be something we can
do?

YURI
Yes, play *Scrabble*. It is your move.

DMITRY
I am not sure I can concentrate
anymore, I am a bit angry and annoyed
with those English rats...

> *(Dmitry looks at his rack of
> letters and starts to pick them
> up.)*

...Oh, what is this? Yes.
J.E.T.P.A.C.K.S - 'Jetpacks' - that is
triple letter score on 'J' tile, that
is 24 + 1 is 25,26,29,33,36,41 + 1 = 45
+ 50 bonus points for 8 letter word =
95 points. That is not as good as last
time, but not bad considering my mood.
Your turn.

> *(Yuri looks at his tiles and
> shakes his head.)*

YURI
T.E.A - 'Tea' - that is 3,4 + 1 = 5.
Five points. I hope I get better
letters this time from bag...

> *(Yuri puts his hand in the
> Scrabble bag and pulls out 2
> letters.)*

...Typical an 'I' and an 'E'. This is
not my finest hour.

                    DMITRY
Don't worry Yuri, I must have had
beginners luck, it is bound to change.
There is plenty of game left to play.

            *(Yuri tops up Dmitry's glass
            and then his own. He lights
            another cigarette and places
            his little tartan friend on the
            side. He is about to sit back
            in his seat when the radio
            begins whistling.)*

                    VLADIMIR
Space Station this is *Mission Control*,
over.

            *(Yuri and Dmitry stay frozen in
            time for a moment.)*

                    YURI
What should we do, Dmitry?

                    DMITRY
Just listen for a moment.

            *(There is a brief silence and
            then the radio comes on again.)*

                    VLADIMIR
This is *Mission Control* calling
International Space Station, is there
anyone still alive up there?

            *(The Radio channel has been
            left open and voices can be

heard in the background.)

                    VOICE 1
...I am telling you they are all dead.
The *Space Station* would have no life
support by now...

                    VOICE 2
...if we wait for C.L.A.R.S.A.C.H.S to
send up their laser to pierce Dome, we
can secretly launch a missile through
eye of storm...

                    VOICE 3
...I agree, it is better to wait. If
we act before we think, it will only
make matters worse. Why launch a
missile that will be seen when we can
hide it inside that laser beam...

                    VOICE 4
...Why is the *Space Station* still
there? Why didn't the explosives
destroy it?

                    VLADIMIR
We don't know sir, we are still trying
to get clear images and reliable
data...

        *(The Radio whistles and goes
        dead.)*

                    YURI
What are we going to do Dmitry? I

thought I might fall asleep and die of
Cerebral Hypoxia, not be blown apart.
I don't mind telling you Dmitry, I am a
little scared.

DMITRY
Relax Yuri, it will be alright. What
did they mean, pierce Dome? I think
your aunt and uncle may have been doing
a bit more than building schools at
Cammachmore.

YURI
I think they also mentioned a casino,
but I can't be sure.

DMITRY
How much time do we have before they
fire off that laser?

YURI
That Professor MacTavish said they were
going to launch the laser at teatime,
Scottish time.

DMITRY
Erm, what is that? Let me see, they
are two hours behind us, what time will
that be?

YURI
A little after 2 o'clock Russian time.

DMITRY
That gives us about seven hours.

                    YURI
To do what?

                   DMITRY
To release the locking clamps that are
keeping us attached to Dome cables.

                    YURI
What good will that do? We will fall
to Earth and be squashed like bug on
windscreen of car - Splat!

     *(Yuri reaches for his little
     tartan trousered friend and
     takes a cigarette and lights
     it. His hands are shaking.)*

                   DMITRY
We will pass out before impact and will
not feel or know anything.

                    YURI
It seems a little radical Dmitry?

                   DMITRY
The way I see it, is like this. We can
wait around for next seven hours and be
blown apart, or we can have the best
fairground ride money can buy... but
the best part, the best part, is that
those English rats and our corrupt
Russian government will be exposed.
When they find *International Space
Station* and 3 mangled bodies all over
some farmer's field, there will be a

lot of explaining to do, especially if we leave recorded message about explosive devices and English cowardliness. It would also clear our tarnished names.

> (*Yuri takes a long puff of his cigarette.*)

                    YURI
We would have to go to the other 3 sectors of *Station* to release clamps. That would mean a 2 man job, 2 for you and 2 for me...

> (*Yuri puts out his cigarette.*)

...we could do the Russian quarters last and retreat back in here for a great view out of window.

                  DMITRY
If we do sections 1 and 3 simultaneously at same time, within a millisecond, and I mean a millisecond, *Station* should not move. Then repeat process for 2 and 4, but with a two minute timer delay giving me enough time to get back here. We should get nice straight flight back to Earth with best seat in house...

> (*Dmitry takes a drink of vodka.*)

...suit up Yuri we have work to do.

                    YURI
What about game, shall we call it a
draw?

                   DMITRY
Under normal conditions I might laugh
in your face, but we are not under
normal conditions. Let's call it a
draw.

Scene fades.

ACT 3, SCENE 1

It has been over six hours since Dmitry and Yuri heard from *Mission Control*. They have tidied up their quarters and removed everything out into the hall. They have bolted two seats to the floor directly in front of the window looking out to Earth. A bottle of vodka is on the floor by Dmitry's seat and Yuri's little tartan bear sits in his seat. They are now wearing their space suits and preparing to leave their quarters.

DMITRY
You remember codes for clamp, yes?

YURI
Yes, they are 1,5,7,...J,K,...4,F and erm, I think it's a 4 next, followed by a Q, no wait that is not it, it's Y then Q... and the next code is...

DMITRY
Take this felt pen and write codes on arm of space suit so you will not have to remember them.

(*Yuri takes the pen and writes down the codes.*)

YURI
It's a pity you did not show me pen thirty minutes ago, I have a headache now.

                    DMITRY
Now, remember... Go to sector 3 first
and enter code, but don't press green
activate button. When I have contacted
you, and given you countdown from
three, press green button and I will do
same in sector 1. If everything goes
to plan, we shouldn't move about too
much. Quickly make your way back here
and enter code and wait for me to call
you. Remember to put in a time delay
of two minutes. We can keep in contact
using our voice COM.

                    YURI
I think I have it...

        (Yuri holds out his hand to
        Dmitry and they shake.)

...the best of luck.

        (Dmitry and Yuri leave their
        quarters and open the hatch to
        the other sectors. Yuri pulls
        himself along the corridor
        towards section 3 and Dmitry
        leaves for section 1. They
        both arrive at the support
        clamp interfaces about 5
        minutes later.)

                    DMITRY
Are you there yet, Yuri?

        (Yuri moves a metal grid and
        some pipes out of the way and

arrives at the interface.)

                    YURI
Yes, I am here. I am entering code as
we speak.

                   DMITRY
Good, I will do same.

                    YURI
... Y. Q... That's it I have done it.
The green light is on.

                   DMITRY
Good. On my mark. 3. 2. 1. Press it
Yuri.

                    YURI
It is done.

        *(A sound like steam from an
        iron is heard and a metal
        grinding noise starts above
        them. A screeching unfolds
        into life and begins to
        reverberate around the Station
        only to give way to a deep
        morbid groan denoting agony and
        despair. A gentle sway
        commences and the Station moves
        down slightly and a lasting
        single note of suffering cries
        out into the darkness.)*

DMITRY
Quickly Yuri, get back to Russian
sector and we will do same there.

YURI

Okay, Dmitry.

(*The Space Station continues to
groan and complain. Dmitry
makes his way to sector 2 and
Yuri makes his way back into
the Russian quarters.*)

YURI
Dmitry, I am ready. I have entered code
and set time delay for two minutes.

(*Dmitry arrives at sector 2 and
enters his code.*)

DMITRY
Okay, Yuri. I am here. I am ready - 3.
2. 1. Press it Yuri. Now get back to
your seat as fast as possible.)

YURI
Okay, See you soon.

(*Yuri gets back to their
quarters and straps himself
into the seat. He removes his
gloves and his helmet and takes
out a cigarette. Dmitry enters
their quarters shortly
afterwards, gets in his seat
and straps himself in. He then*

*removes his gloves and helmet
and has a drink of vodka.)*

                    YURI
How much time Dmitry?

                    DMITRY
Another twenty seconds.

          *(Outside the window the storm
          below is more violent than
          ever. A huge whirlpool is seen
          over Russian soil spreading
          outwards towards Europe.)*

                    YURI
Look at that Dmitry, look at what we
are heading into.

                    DMITRY
It will be a bumpy ride for sure.   It
was a pleasure knowing you Yuri.

                    YURI
You too, Dmitry.

          *(The 3rd clamp half releases
          from the American sector and a
          scraping metal sound is heard
          followed by a loud crunch of
          gears and an alarm. Yuri and
          Dmitry get a violent jolt and
          the movement suddenly stops.)*

                    YURI
What has happened, Dmitry?

                    DMITRY
The gear is jammed in the American
Sector and it has failed completely in
the Russian section.

          *(More groaning and crunching,
          followed by scraping. Yuri
          looks out of the window.)*

                    YURI
What the hell is that coming towards
us?

          *(From out of the storm a
          missile is seen heading towards
          them.)*

                    DMITRY
It is a missile, Yuri. Goodbye old
friend!

          *(Suddenly a tremendous blue
          light shoots out from the eye
          of the storm and reaches up to
          the Dome above them.)*

                    YURI
Dmitry, look! They have fired laser.

          *(A big crunch is heard and the
          clamp from sector 3 breaks
          free. The Space Station,
          supported now only by one*

*cable, begins swaying violently
back and forth like a pendulum.
The missile launched from the
surface is about to make
contact.)*

DMITRY

Hold on Yuri.

*(A loud sound like an aircraft
flying close by is heard.)*

YURI

It missed! It missed Dmitry, you can
open your eyes.

DMITRY

What? arrgghh!

*(The Space Station begins to
sway violently towards a big
blue ribbon of light that is
being fired from Earth. Yuri
and Dmitry have a bird's eye
view.)*

YURI

Look at that Dmitry, it must be a
hundred feet wide.

DMITRY

At least. Looks like I was right,
they've been doing a bit more than
building schools in the last 25 years
at Cammachmore.

(The Space Station swings back the other way and is picking up speed. Yuri and Dmitry are now gripping their seats tightly and look distressed.)

YURI

Arrggghhh! This is quite nauseating, the way the Earth is moving so fast, back and forth.

DMITRY

Try and focus on one thing.

(The Space Station goes to a full arc and then heads towards the blue ribbon of light at a great velocity.)

DMITRY

Hold on!

(The Space Station reaches its maximum movement towards the blue ribbon of light and breaks free. It spins round and around and enters the ribbon. Yuri and Dmitry have their eyes closed - then the spinning stops.)

DMITRY

Yuri, open your eyes, it is beautiful, quite magnificent, even ethereal.

(Yuri starts to open his eyes

slowly.)

                    YURI
Dmitry, what's happening? Why aren't
we falling.

                  DMITRY
We are in laser beam, it is great blue
ribbon of light. Look! We are going
up to the top of the Dome, the laser is
punching a hole through it and
expelling the storm. We are heading
for outer space. We are going to be
real cosmonauts Yuri.

                    YURI
Then what?

        (The Space Station is now
        hurtling towards the Dome.
        Inside the ribbon the weather
        is calm and no vibrations can
        be felt. A field of
        electricity surrounds the
        Station and the hole in the
        Dome above them is pulsating in
        size.)

                  DMITRY
We... We... ah, I see your point. Well
at least we did not get blown up.

        (The top of the Dome appears
        and the hole is big enough for
        the Space Station to pass
        through, but then the blue

*ribbon starts to fluctuate in
power and the hole rapidly
changes in size.)*

                    YURI
Oh, no! The light is failing, we are
not going to make it.

                    DMITRY
We are almost there.

          *(The ribbon powers down and the
          storm around them dissipates.
          The hole in the Dome is
          shrinking at a rapid rate and
          their speed is starting to
          drop.)*

                    YURI
C'mon, you piece of junk, just a few
more feet.

          *(They approach the Dome as the
          hole is closing and just make
          it through. The Dome seals the
          gap behind them and they are
          now in space. The Space
          Station starts to spin and
          rotate moving a few hundred
          yards passed the Dome then
          stops. Yuri, Dmitry and the
          Space Station are now floating
          in real space.)*

                    DMITRY
We are through Yuri, we made it!

*(Yuri looks around and his
little tartan friend is
floating about in their
quarters along with helmets,
gloves and a bottle of vodka.)*

YURI

Dmitry, we are floating, look at bear.
I feel weightless Dmitry, just like in
pool but much drier.

DMITRY

Yuri, we are true cosmonaut. The first
people in history of our planet to pass
through Dome and to make it into outer
space.

YURI

It is a shame that no one will know.
They would have made statues, named
high schools after us and put name down
in history book...

*(Dmitry is transfixed on the
window looking out to their new
world and his mouth is open.
Yuri looks across to Dmitry.)*

...Dmitry, why is your mouth open?

(Dmitry points at the window.)

DMITRY

Look! Look! Look, Yuri!

(Yuri looks out the window.)

                    YURI
What is that? It is gigantic, it must
be a mile wide. It is just hanging
there.

          (Yuri and Dmitry are looking
          out at an alien spaceship that
          sits just above the Dome.)

                    DMITRY
It is alien ship... It is ship that
has been in my life for so long, but I
never thought I would actually see it
in flesh. Look at it Yuri, it is over
5000 years old. It is a menace, an
evil thing of unknown origin. It sits
there like a big black monstrous
creature slowly killing its prey...

          (Dmitry releases his belt and
          floats over to the window.)

...Look at hull, the metal is thick and
rough like bad welding at shipyard.
Who knows what secrets lie within Yuri.

          (Yuri unbuckles his belt and
          floats over to the window next
          to Dmitry.)

                    YURI
It is horrible black mess like bubbling
bitumen on road. It is difficult to
make out shapes, just shades of black

in black background. It looks demonic - a real Pandora's box. I would not like to venture over there.   'Death awaits all who enter', I bet it says that on door...

(An alarm sounds and part of
the Space Station breaks off
and floats away.)

...What now, what is happening?

                    DMITRY
The hull is weakening, we are losing life support and cabin pressure. Quick, get on your space suit and put as much food and equipment into one of the containers in the corridor. We have to get out of here.

                    YURI
What do you mean? Where are we going to go? Shall I call a cab?

                    DMITRY
We shall have to take our chances over there.

                    YURI
What on that thing, we will surely die?

(The window in their quarters
starts to crack.)

                    DMITRY
Quick there is no time for debate, we

must go.

> (The *Space Station* starts to
> collapse. Yuri and Dmitry have
> their space suits on and are
> seen moving through the
> corridors with a big container.
> Debris, wires, bits of plastic
> and metal float around.
> Crunching, scraping and
> groaning and bursting sounds
> can be heard.)

YURI
The hatch is stuck Dmitry!

> (Dmitry grabs a floating bar
> and levers it open. They move
> inside a pressure chamber and
> wait for the other door to
> activate for release.)

DMITRY
C'mon, just open before we are crushed
like bug on shoe.

> (The door releases and they are
> outside floating in space.
> They are seen moving away from
> the Space Station with a big
> storage container between them.
> As they get further away using
> their jetpacks the Space
> Station implodes.)

Scene fades.

ACT 3. SCENE 2

Yuri and Dmitry are now floating in space and observe the crushed Space Station with an air of chagrin and alarm. Between them, they are carrying a large storage container filled with supplies. Below, the Earth is clearly in view and storm Ivan has dissipated to a few white cirrocumulus clouds and the skies are bright blue. The Dome, for the first time, is seen from the other side, encompassing the Earth with a diaphanous film of liquid electricity that is visible for a second then disappears, only to reappear again. Ahead of Dmitry and Yuri lies the alien spaceship - a big black monster.

DMITRY

That was a close thing, we nearly got crumpled.

YURI

I think you mean minced! Now what is plan?

DMITRY

Plan? Who said anything about plan? I just thought we should get out of *Space Station*. That was as far as my plan went...

(*Dmitry looks into the distance at the* alien spaceship *and then down at his air supply gauge.*)

...How much air do you have?

                    YURI
About 45 minutes.

                    DMITRY
Good. Here is plan. We are going to
make our way over to alien spaceship
and see if we can get inside.

                    YURI
Dmitry, we don't know anything about
ship, we could be walking into instant
death.

                    DMITRY
What would you like to do? In 44
minutes you will be dead if you stay
here. Now, ship is further away than
it looks, I suggest we get started.

                    YURI
After reflection, I think you are right
Dmitry, we should get to ship and see
what happens.

                    DMITRY
Good, let's go.

          (They fire off their jetpacks
          and start heading towards the
          alien spaceship.)

                    YURI
Dmitry, now we are away from *Space*

Station, why don't we speak in our
mother tongue?

                    DMITRY
I would prefer it if we did not, I am
alright with speaking English.

                    YURI
Okay, but I thought it would be nice.
We have always communicated with each
other in a foreign language, and I have
never heard you speak much Russian?

        (*Dmitry looks a little
        uncomfortable behind the
        protection of his helmet.*)

                    DMITRY
The truth is Yuri, my Russian is not
too good.

                    YURI
What? You are Dmitry Usakov, Russian
cosmonaut. What do you mean your
Russian is not too good?

                    DMITRY
There is a lot you don't know about me
Yuri.

                    YURI
Like what?

                    DMITRY
I don't know if this is right time or

place.

YURI
I might be dead in 32 minutes time,
it's now or never!

DMITRY
Well, when I was a little boy, my
parents told me not to speak Russian
anymore. They said I was to be part of
secret programme and that I needed to
speak English only and forget my
Russian upbringing. I had just turned
7 at this point. A year later my
parents took me to train station, put
me on train and said goodbye. It would
be 8 long years before I saw them
again.

YURI
8 years, you must have travelled a
great distance, I did not know railway
line was so long. What did you do for
food?

DMITRY
I was not on train for 8 years! I was
at school for boys with special
abilities.

YURI
You must have known my cousin Yurak, he
went to same school, he had a speech
impediment and stuttered all the time.
The teachers there tried to train him
to say: 'Sleazy Sally Satchel Smoothly

Slithers and Slides Shaking Salt Sachets.', but he always got stuck on 'Sachets', and he never advanced in class. It is a bit of a tongue twister without problem of stutter. You must have done better than him to get home so soon, he was 26 before he could leave. He now works as cultural minister for Russia.

> *(Up ahead in the distance the big black monster gets closer and starts to take on a more uniform shape.)*

                    DMITRY
I said special abilities, not special needs!

                    YURI
What is difference?

                    DMITRY
One means to be blessed with exceptional qualities and have an aptitude for things, and the other means you have a disability of some kind.

                    YURI
So, you were clever child?

                    DMITRY
Yes.

                    YURI
Then why can you not speak Russian very
well?

                    DMITRY
Sometimes Yuri, there is no point in
talking to you. You are an
insufferable companion.

                    YURI
Insufferable? That is a big word
coming from somebody who can't even
speak his mother tongue.

                    DMITRY
I did not say I could not speak it, I
am a little rusty that is all. You did
not even let me finish story, you had
to interject with stupid tale about
your cousin Yurak. If we die here, at
least I won't have to listen to any
more of your stupid stories!

                    YURI
I see, it is like that. Stupid
stories? Insufferable? You didn't
mind my company when you were stuffing
your face with my lamb stew. You are
hypocrite. A self-important nobody,
who inflates his reality to feel like
he is big man. Russian cosmonaut, my
foot, you are a drunkard with a temper
and a cold heart. I have had to clean
up your mess since this trek started.
If it wasn't for me and my mouse you
would be dead by now...

*(Yuri's air supply starts to
fail and he starts to
hyperventilate. Dmitry lets go
of the container and moves
closer to Yuri.)*

                    DMITRY
Yuri, stay calm. You are running out
of air.

          *(Dmitry pulls a cable from his
          side and attaches it to Yuri's
          air supply. Slowly Yuri stops
          hyperventilating and begins to
          breathe normally.)*

                    YURI
That is better. Thank you Dmitry. I
am sorry, I couldn't help myself, I
didn't know what I was saying.

                    DMITRY
It is alright, your brain was suffering
from a lack of oxygen and was having a
meltdown. Even so, some of what you
said was true. We don't have much time
Yuri. We only have 20 minutes of air.

          *(They grab the container and
          put their jetpacks on full
          power. They shoot across the
          blackness of space and arrive
          at the alien spaceship.)*

                    DMITRY
It is certainly big, it could take days

to find an entrance into this thing,
maybe even weeks!

                    YURI
There must be a way in. Look Dmitry!
I think it's a door. Look it is huge,
massive great big hatch... but we can't
use it.

                    DMITRY
Why?

                    YURI
There is message on door.

                    DMITRY
What does it say?

                    YURI
'Death awaits all who enter.'

        (They both laugh.)

                    DMITRY
I can't believe you are fooling around
at a time like this, we only have 10
minutes of air left.

        (Yuri looks at the door,
        presses a button and grabs a
        lever on the hatch. A sound of
        compressed air escaping is
        heard and the door opens.)

                    DMITRY
Yuri, you have done it. Quickly let's
get inside.

          (Dmitry, Yuri and their
          container enter the alien
          spaceship through a big black
          door. It closes behind them
          with a loud clunk that
          reverberates down a vast
          tunnel. It is dark and damp.
          Water droplets drip continually
          from the tunnel's roof, which
          is over 30 feet high. The only
          light is coming from the torch
          on their helmets.)

                    DMITRY
Look Yuri? It is vast, I can't see an
end to it.

          (Dmitry and Yuri are still in a
          zero gravity atmosphere and are
          still floating above the tunnel
          floor.)

                    YURI
Dmitry, I am not feeling too good.

                    DMITRY
You are almost out of air. Let's go
along this tunnel as fast as we can,
there must be a way in to ship
interior.

          (They fire off their jetpacks

and zoom down the tunnel at
great speed and arrive at
another big door. The door has
buttons and a lever. Yuri is
starting to gasp for air.)

                    YURI
Hurry Dmitry, I can't breathe.

                    DMITRY
What to press?...

        (Dmitry presses some buttons
        and the door opens.)

...That's it.

        (Dmitry grabs Yuri and they get
        inside of a chamber. A loud
        siren is heard and the door
        closes. The sound of air
        gushing through pipes can be
        heard and then lights start to
        activate in the chamber - first
        one, then another, and then
        another, until it is very
        bright.)

                    YURI
I can't breathe, Dmitry help me?

                    DMITRY
Don't worry, take off your helmet, the
chamber has pressurised.

                    YURI
But what if air... What if air... Air
is poison?

                    DMITRY
We shall soon see.

          *(Dmitry twists, then pulls off
          Yuri's Helmet. Yuri takes a
          big breath of air and collapses
          on the floor.)*

                    YURI
You could have killed me. What if air
was poison?

                    DMITRY
Then I would have robbed you of 30
seconds of life...

          *(Yuri is still recovering on
          the floor.)*

...How is air?

                    YURI
It is very stale, like old rubber tyre,
but breathable. Better than
alternative.

                    DMITRY
Good...

          (Dmitry removes his helmet.)

...Yes, quite stale, but I will take

it.

(Yuri gets to his feet.)

YURI
Zero gravity has gone, I feel heavy. I
will take this as a good sign. Now we
are inside belly of beast, what is
plan?

DMITRY
Why is there always need for plan? We
are here, we are alive. Let's just
take a moment to reflect on situation,
catch our breath and take a seat for
five minutes. Let's move container
over there and we will have a think.

(Dmitry and Yuri go to lift the
container, but it now seems
quite heavy.)

YURI
Why is it so heavy?

DMITRY
We have lost zero gravity...

(Dmitry grunts.)

...There. That will do.

(They both sit on the container
dangling their feet like school
boys at the harbour fishing for
Mackerel. Yuri reaches inside

his space suit and pulls out
his little tartan friend.)

                    DMITRY
I can't believe you still have bear,
even in panic of *Space Station*
evacuation you have time to grab bear.

                    YURI
I like a smoke; it is very relaxing and
helps me think...

        (Yuri reaches inside his space
        suit again.)

... I have just remembered something.

        (He hands Dmitry a half bottle
        of Brandy.)

                    DMITRY
Yuri, you are a true friend. Things
are definitely looking up.

        (Dmitry takes a good drink and
        then passes it to Yuri. A puff
        of smoke fills the air then
        Yuri takes a good drink.)

                    YURI
Dmitry, do you think there is anyone
here, on board this ship after all
these years?

        (Yuri passes Dmitry the bottle
        of brandy.)

                    DMITRY
I don't know, but if there is, they
would be aware of our presence by now.
It is probably best that we didn't stay
here too long. We can't take this
trunk with us, it's too heavy. We will
have to take the bare essentials and
that's it.

          (They sit for a few moments
          longer then go through the
          container. They take out some
          bits of food, water and some
          tools, a laser cutter, a multi-
          spanner, a pack of cigarettes
          and a small bottle of whisky.)

                    DMITRY
C'mon Yuri, let's see what this ship
has on board - good or bad.

          (Yuri stuffs a can of tuna, two
          cartons of cigarettes, 5 cooked
          sausages, some apples, a video
          camera and an explosive device
          down his trousers.)

                    YURI
Okay, I am right behind you.

          (Dmitry pulls the lever on the
          hatch door and it opens. They
          both walk through and it closes
          behind them.)

Scene fades.

ACT 3, SCENE 3

The scene opens in a vast corridor leading in two directions - to the left, the corridor disappears into the distance and seems to be endless. To the right, it looks the same but slightly cleaner. The corridor is depressing and in a state of dereliction. A lime green paint peels from the top part of the walls and a wooden panelled bottom half is faded and split in several places. Orange domed light fittings hang from the ceiling on chain cables and fluorescent tubes dangle like forgotten Christmas decorations. Plaster lies on the floor and water droplets form on mouldy crusty metal sconces with half burnt candles. It is dark except for Dmitry and Yuri's torch lights that they carry in their hands.

                    YURI
This is very strange, I might even say surreal. This looks like a bad seventies hotel left to rot. This must have been the servants walk way to access major parts of ship. Which way shall we go?

                   DMITRY
Let's go this way, it doesn't look quite as bad.

          (Dmitry and Yuri choose to walk

*down the corridor on their
right.)*

                    YURI
This looks like it's been abandoned for
a long time Dmitry...

          *(Yuri peels off some paint from
          the wall.)*

...They might be all dead by now.
After all, this ship has been here for
5,000 years.

          *(Yuri sees what appears to be a
          light switch and flicks it.
          Lights come on along the
          corridor. The orange domed
          lights and the dangling
          fluorescent tubes burst into
          life. Dmitry turns around
          quickly.)*

                    DMITRY
Arrgh! You gave me a scare... Next
time, tell me if you are going to touch
something.

          *(Everywhere is bright, but very
          depressing. Everything is
          falling apart and dilapidated.
          Everything smells mouldy.)*

                    YURI
Sorry, but at least we can see.

DMITRY

Turn off your torchlight, it will save
battery.

YURI

Okay - What a dump, what do you make of
it?

DMITRY

It is too early to say, it is certainly
a surprise, but it was always going to
be that. It is probably best to
reserve judgement until we have seen
more of ship and reconnoitred a little
further. I just hope we manage to get
to end of corridor before legs become
tired.

> (Dmitry and Yuri walk for
> another 10 minutes with no sign
> of an exit. The corridor
> appears to have no end.
> Varying states of decay denote
> the only change in their
> current surroundings.)

YURI

I think I will have a drink of water
and a cigarette. Can we stop for a
minute?

DMITRY

Okay, but can I ask you something that
has been troubling me for a while?

                    YURI
Sure, anything?

                    DMITRY
Are you sure your mother did not steal
chickens?

          (Yuri takes a swig of water and
          spits it out and then looks
          over to Dmitry.)

                    YURI
You are crazy Dmitry, we are stuck on
alien spaceship, and you are still
obsessing about 15 year old chicken
mystery. Okay, Quid Pro Quo?

                    DMITRY
What?

                    YURI

You tell me something that I want to
know, and in return, I will tell you
what I know about chickens.

                    DMITRY
So, you do know something. Okay, what
do you want to know?

          (Yuri takes out a cigarette
          from his little tartan friend,
          lights it and begins to smoke.)

                    YURI
You were 8 years old, you travelled on
train for many miles and found yourself
at school for special children. You
returned home 8 years later, what
happened in those 8 years?

                   DMITRY
Now you are interested. Okay, I will
tell you. The school I was sent to was
a place not on map, but hidden in heart
of Siberia. The school was situated in
middle of exact replica of English
town, known as Oxford. The government
were running special covert operations
in England, planting spies and sleepers
to act as a liaison for new recruits.
This enabled hundreds of Russian agents
to learn culture, speak language and
get genuine feel for country.

                    YURI
Sounds very clandestine. So, you
became a spy for Russia?

                   DMITRY
Not exactly. I could not learn accent
so they sent me back home.

                    YURI
It took them eight years to find out
you could not learn accent?

                   DMITRY
No, that only took a couple of months.
I knew I would be big embarrassment to

parents if I went back home, so I
begged school to keep me on as Tea boy.

                    YURI
A Tea boy?...

        (Yuri starts to laugh out
        loud.)

...A Tea boy. That is funniest thing I
have heard. You a Tea boy.

                    DMITRY
What is funny about that?

        (Yuri is still laughing.)

                    YURI
I have had your tea, you always rip bag
open and put milk in pot. Dmitry, you
can't make tea, you don't know how.

                    DMITRY
You are jackass Yuri, I confide in you
something I have never told anyone and
you laugh in my face. You are
insensitive and cruel... Now, tell me
about chicken?

        (Yuri is still laughing. He has
        a last drag of his cigarette
        and throws it on floor, then
        puts it out with his foot.)

                    YURI
C'mon, let's get going and I will tell

you about chicken...

(They start walking again.)

...My mother never stole chicken, it
was my father. Every Thursday my
father would take truck and drive it to
your father's chicken factory and pay
one of the warehouse men to look other
way while he loaded up truck with fresh
chicken. My mother never knew, she had
always given my father money to buy
wholesale chickens but he always blew
it on beer and racetrack. I have kept
that secret from my mother all these
years and I expect you to do same. If
we get back, I will send your father a
cheque for chickens. Now, enough about
chickens.

                    DMITRY
I knew it. I have always known it. I
knew that you knew...

        *(Up ahead the Corridor comes to
        an end, no door, just a dead
        end.)*

...and now I know it for sure.

                    YURI
Well, I am happy for you Dmitry. I am
sure you will sleep easy tonight
knowing what you know.

        *(Dmitry and Yuri are now at the
        end of the corridor and there*

*is just a wall that looks the
same as everywhere else.)*

DMITRY
This is not good, this is bad. I don't
fancy that walk back... What if the
other way's the same?

YURI
Walk a bit further, right up to wall.

*(Dmitry gets closer to the wall
and it opens upwards showing a
small room that looks like a
lift.)*

DMITRY
Yuri, I don't know where I'd be without
you.

(Yuri looks into the lift.)

YURI
I don't like the look of that elevator,
it looks rotten. All of the metal has
corroded. It might not even work.

*(Before them is an octagonal
shaped room made from metal and
wood. Various decorative
designs cover the border of
seven wooden panels and a
chandelier hangs down from the
centre of the ceiling. To the
left of the door is a brass
panel with 50 green buttons and*

> *one big orange button at the*
> *top.)*

DMITRY
Well, there is only one way to find
out, I am past caring, my legs are
tired and I want a bath!

YURI
I am willing to give it a try if you
are?

> *(They both get inside and the*
> *wall panel comes down.)*

YURI
What buttons shall we press?

DMITRY
Press the top green button.

> *(Yuri presses the top green*
> *button.)*

YURI
Nothing is happening, it's a dud!

DMITRY
Try that big orange button.

YURI
Okay.

> *(Yuri presses the button and*
> *the lift begins to move*

upwards.)

                    DMITRY
That's it Yuri, we are moving!

          *(The lift climbs upwards. At
          first it is very slow, but soon
          picks up speed and gets very
          fast. A groaning, crunching,
          metal scraping sound repeats
          along the side as they ascend.)*

                    YURI
It's getting very fast Dmitry.

                    DMITRY
Yes, we are really flying now. Finally
we are getting somewhere.

          *(The lift gets even faster and
          they both hold on to the walls.
          The speed begins to decrease
          and finally comes to a stop.
          The wall panel lifts up and
          they are now in a big room full
          of rectangular units with reel
          to reel tape machines mounted
          on them. Everywhere is orange
          and white.)*

                    YURI
What is this place? Looks like my
grandfather's old tape collection. He
was a great one for recording
conversations.

*(They enter the room and walk
amongst the units.)*

                    DMITRY
Was he interested in archiving your
family's history?

                    YURI
No, nothing like that. He would record
conversations between married men and
their girlfriends.

                    DMITRY
What for?

                    YURI
On the pretence of obtaining money. He
would tell them he would play tape for
wife if they did not pay him to keep it
a secret.

                    DMITRY
Your grandfather was a blackmailer!

          *(In the room, the reel to reel
          tapes spin and whizz around
          making chirping noises. Yuri
          and Dmitry continue to walk
          through the maze of units.)*

                    YURI
Not really. He never took any money.

                    DMITRY
I don't understand?

                    YURI
Well, he would tell husband that he
wanted 80,000 Rubles or he would hand
tape to wife. When husband was away at
bank or trying to borrow money from
friends, my grandfather would give tape
to wife for her to play. When the
husband came home, there would be a big
row and husband would be thrown out.

                    DMITRY
I don't get it?

                    YURI
Well, my grandfather liked a good
laugh. When he dropped off tape to
wife, he would bug the house. Later at
night he would play back recording and
laugh over couple's plight.

                    DMITRY
Your grandfather was sick, with a
sadistic nature. How did you find out
about it?

                    YURI
He used to play tapes for family to
hear every Sunday when we had roast
dinner.

                    DMITRY
Your grandfather was quite macabre, I
would even say ghoulish.

YURI

Well, he is dead now, so why does it
matter.

DMITRY

How did he die?

YURI

He choked on a chicken bone. It was a
nice big chicken my father had got for
us for Sunday lunch. My grandfather
played tape for us all to listen to and
he was finding it funny, well, we all
thought it was funny, and then he
started to choke on bone. We tried
everything to get it out, even the
vacuum cleaner, but nothing worked.
Even when he was choking he was still
laughing. My mother had to throw tea
towel over his face to hide strange
expression of suffering and joy. My
father suggested we put him in lounge
while we finished dinner.

DMITRY

You carried on eating dinner when your
grandfather had just died?

YURI

What can I say, it was a tasty chicken,
it would have been crime to waste it.

> (*The sea of rectangular units
> and tape reels had come to a
> sudden stop and a large cart
> carrying cartons of valves the*

*size of balloons drove past
following a yellow line on the
floor.)*

                    DMITRY
What is this now? Yuri have you ever
seen a valve that big?

                    YURI
No, but I have not seen a valve for
years. We used to have an old wireless
set in spare bedroom, but it did not
have valves that size.

                    DMITRY
This ship is very odd. All of the
technology seems 20th century, and the
decor is out of some bad 1970's motel.

                    YURI
Why don't we follow this cart for a
while, it must have a purpose.

                    DMITRY
I can't suggest anything better, so
let's do it.

        *(Dmitry and Yuri follow the
        cart until it disappears into a
        room. They follow the cart and
        now stand at the entrance to a
        vast room full of boxes of
        valves. The cart empties the
        valves on the floor and leaves
        back through the door.)*

                    DMITRY

Did you ever see such a thing? There
must be millions of valves in here,
maybe even billions. All different
sizes and shapes.

                     YURI

But what's it all for? Nobody uses
valves anymore. There must be 10 or
twenty here for everyone on planet
below. It doesn't make any sense.

                    DMITRY

C'mon let's get going, there must be
something on this ship we can grasp.
All I know is that a power source of
some kind is keeping that Dome in
place. We must find it and turn it
off. Our best course of action is to
try and find bridge.

          *(Dmitry and Yuri walk for
          another 30 minutes along a huge
          open space like an empty
          warehouse and come to a large
          door at the end. The door is
          gold in colour and looks very
          solid and heavy. At the side
          there is a panel with what
          looks like symbols.)*

                     YURI

My legs are tired, I hope there is
chair behind door.

                    DMITRY
We shall have to get through it first.
It might be a tough nut to crack.

                    YURI
Try pressing button that looks like
Kielbasa sausage.

                    DMITRY
Why that one, why not the one that
looks like a chilli pepper?

                    YURI
I am not in mood for spicy food.

          (They both laugh.)

                    YURI
You choose, what does it matter.

          *(Dmitry studies the buttons and
          presses a symbol that looks
          like an 'E'. Nothing happens.)*

                    DMITRY
I don't think this console is working?

                    YURI
Just press all of them, and see what
happens?

          *(Dmitry starts to press all of
          the buttons and a loud droning
          noise sounds throughout the
          room. Gear noises crunch and a*

*big boom rings out. In the
distance a large metal plate
falls to the floor and
reverberates around the
chamber.)*

                    YURI
I don't think this is good, what is
that?

          *(In the distance, where the
          plate had fallen, an enormous
          metal figure comes into sight.
          Dmitry is still trying the
          buttons on the console without
          success.)*

                    YURI
What are you doing, have you seen this
thing?

          *(A huge machine is moving
          towards them. It is shaped
          like a bomb disposal device and
          has many moving turrets. Red
          laser beams are now searching
          the chamber and appear to be
          scanning for life forms.)*

                    YURI
Hurry up, this thing is getting closer.

                    DMITRY
I have pressed all of the buttons, what
would you like me to do?

                    YURI
Quick, get out of way.

          *(Yuri grabs a large screwdriver
          from a pocket on his trouser
          leg and prises off the panel.
          Behind it he finds a mess of
          covered cables and thin yellow
          wires, two of the wires seem to
          be broken.)*

                  DMITRY
Holy hotdog stand! This thing is as
big as a dumper truck. How is it
coming with that panel?

                    YURI
I am joining these two wires back
together. Look, the chilli pepper
button has lit up.

                  DMITRY
Looks like we are eating hot and spicy
after all.

          *(Dmitry presses the chilli
          pepper symbol and the gold door
          starts to open. Gears start to
          crunch. It opens slightly then
          gets stuck.)*

                    YURI
It is stuck, what luck!

          (The big machine is closing in

*on them and is still scanning
the area.)*

                    DMITRY
I think it is good enough, see if you
can squeeze through.

          *(Gears crunch and the door
          begins to open wider.)*

                    YURI
That's it! C'mon, let's get out of
here.

          *(The machine's lasers locate
          Dmitry and Yuri and it starts
          firing a pulse weapon in their
          direction. Dmitry squeezes
          through the door and Yuri yanks
          the yellow wires apart and gets
          through as well. The door
          closes. They fall to the
          ground. They are now in an
          area that looks like an airport
          terminal, lots of check-in
          kiosks and shop fronts, all
          with a 1970's feel about them.
          There is blank signage
          everywhere conveying nothing.)*

                    DMITRY
That was a narrow escape, I am glad we
are on this side of door...

          *(Yuri stands up and looks
          around. Everywhere is well*

> *illuminated by white domed*
> *ceiling lights.)*

...Where are we now, looks like Anapa
airport terminal in 1970's. This place
is crazy. In my childhood, I dreamed
of getting inside this ship and seeing
all of secrets it would hold.

                    YURI
You knew of ship then?

                    DMITRY
I may have been Tea boy in Siberian
Oxford, but I had access to important
confidential files. I did not spend my
time making tea all the while; I put my
fingers into every sticky jar I could
find.

> *(Yuri brushes himself down and*
> *looks around.)*

                    YURI
Well, I hope at some point that
information helps us get out of this
place.

                    DMITRY
So do I Yuri.

                    YURI
Y'know, this place does look a little
like Anapa airport. I was not there in
the seventies, but I did go there in
1990's.

                    DMITRY
Were you going on holiday somewhere?

                     YURI
No, my cousin Olrig was visiting from
Poland and I went with my parents to
collect him from airport, but he got
arrested and went to jail.

     (Dmitry and Yuri start to walk
     through the airport.)

                    DMITRY
He got arrested, what did he do?

                     YURI
He got caught smuggling cocaine.

                    DMITRY
Cocaine, that is bad. It is difficult
to smuggle narcotics through airport
nowadays with all of the preventative
measures that are taken: baggage X-
rays, metal detecting scans, strip
searches, sniffer dogs, pat-downs...

     (Dmitry looks up at all of the
     blank signage.)

...You would have to be fool to think
you could get away with smuggling drugs
through airport with all that against
you. How did they catch your cousin?

                     YURI
It was his own ineptitude that let him

down...

> (Yuri takes out his tartan
> friend and gets a cigarette.
> He lights it and takes a drag.)

...He had seen a movie where a criminal
had dissolved some cocaine powder into
some masonry paint. Obviously this was
to disguise smell of drug from sniffer
dogs.

DMITRY
Is that what your cousin did?

YURI
No. He had a much better idea. He
decided to rub other passengers'
luggage with beef dripping and bacon
fat.

DMITRY
Beef dripping and bacon fat?

> (Yuri looks around at the empty
> shops.)

YURI
Yes, the plan was misdirection. At
luggage check out, sniffer dogs would
roam airport for drugs, tobacco and
food. Olrig thought if he covered
other passengers' bags with beef
dripping and bacon fat, the dogs would
go after that, and he could walk
straight through airport security while

Customs Officers checked on suspicious
luggage.

DMITRY
Sounds like an original plan, that is
for sure. What happened next?

YURI
He walked straight through security.
He was right, the dogs went crazy over
fatty suitcases. Everything was going
fine until he got to escalator. A
little old lady let go of her dog's
lead and it ran straight to his bag.
In his panic to sully decoy luggage, he
covered his own bag with bacon fat and
beef dripping. The old lady's dog
wouldn't leave his bag alone, so he
pulled it away and bag got caught in
escalator step...

(Yuri puts out his cigarette.)

...At this point, we were already
waving at Olrig from top of escalator,
then the bag exploded open and we were
all covered in cocaine...

*(Yuri looks around at the
various broken shop displays.)*

...My mother took a while to get over
that incident.

DMITRY
I guess it would be quite traumatic and

a bit embarrassing.

                    YURI
She wasn't embarrassed, she had lost
200,000 Rubles in merchandise, and a
valuable member of her distribution
network. It took her months to find
someone else.

          (Dmitry and Yuri continue to
          walk through the airport. It
          is very run down and looks like
          nobody has been there for
          years. Water drops from the
          ceiling and mould and mildew
          cover the majority of the
          furnishings. Up ahead there is
          a big circular seating area.
          All of the furnishings are
          bright orange. White plastic
          is everywhere with dashes of
          geometric patterns of pale
          green and dark brown squares.)

                    DMITRY
Your mother was a drug dealer?

                    YURI
Only for a little while, then she got
into chicken business. Dmitry, let's
sit down, I am exhausted. Those orange
seats look inviting and they don't look
that mouldy.

                    DMITRY
Okay, for a little while.

(Dmitry and Yuri take a seat to rest, but soon fall asleep.)

Scene fades.

ACT 4. SCENE 1

Everywhere is white. Two white beds encompassed in a white moulded frame sit opposite one another and are attached to the walls. The walls are white and the floor is white. The room is seamless and has no doors or windows, no exits can be seen. The room is very clean. A bright white crystal hangs from the ceiling 25 feet up and is the source of light. A small vent is also visible about 15 feet up and next to it appears to be a small white orb with an electronic eye. The floor area is square with rounded corners - exactly 16 feet by 16 feet. Yuri and Dmitry are unconscious on the floor and are still dressed in their space suits. A misty vapour is being expelled from the room when Dmitry starts to wake up.

                    DMITRY
Oh, my head, it feels like I've been hit with a hammer...

          (Dmitry looks around and sees
          Yuri on the floor next to him.)

... Yuri, are you alive. Wake up!

          (Yuri starts to move and
          groans.)

                    YURI
Why is it so bright? Turn down the

lights...

> *(Yuri sits up and looks
> around.)*

... Where are we Dmitry, how did we get
here?

DMITRY

I don't know, but I don't think we can
be alone anymore.

YURI

Why do you say that?

DMITRY

Well, we didn't walk here, so someone
or something must have carried us.

YURI

But why didn't we wake up?

DMITRY

They must have used an odourless gas to
make us unconscious. I saw a mist
creeping into that vent up there when I
woke up.

YURI

I feel so dopey, and my head feels like
I have smacked it against brick wall.
It's too bright, I can't see a thing.

> *(The white crystal above them
> changes to grey and the light*

level drops.)

That is better. Did you find the
dimmer switch Dmitry?

                    DMITRY
No, I did nothing. Somebody must be
listening to us. Well at least they
don't want us dead.

                    YURI
How do you know that?   They may just
want to interrogate us before they chop
off head.

                    DMITRY
I didn't think of that, you have
cheered me up.

          *(Yuri gets to his feet and also
          helps Dmitry up. They look
          around the room.)*

                    YURI
Doesn't seem to be a way out Dmitry.
Looks like we have finally come to end
of road.

                    DMITRY
You might be right this time. I can't
even see a crease anywhere. There is
no sign of a door, not even a panel
with buttons.

                    YURI
Maybe that is a good thing; the last
panel with buttons nearly got us
killed.

                   DMITRY
But at least it was something to work
with...

          (Dmitry tries to find a
          crease.)

...it's useless, everywhere is smooth
and featureless.

          (Dmitry and Yuri pace the room
          aimlessly for a while and then
          sit down on cushioned white
          beds.)

                    YURI
I am quite hungry. There was a nice
piece of brisket in that container
along with some dark ale gravy and new
boiled potatoes.

                   DMITRY
I am a little hungry, but I am more
thirsty than hungry.

                    YURI
I have a bottle of water in my suit.

                   DMITRY
I was thinking of something a little
stronger.

YURI

I have a small bottle of whisky, but I
would prefer it if you were not drunk
right now.

DMITRY

Okay, pass me water. ...What food do
you have?

YURI

I have a turkey and cranberry sandwich
on brown bread or some beef sausages.

DMITRY

Pass me turkey and cranberry sandwich.

          (Yuri hands over the turkey and
          cranberry sandwich and the
          bottle of water. Dmitry drinks
          some water and starts to eat.
          Yuri also eats a sandwich.)

YURI

There is something I have been meaning
to mention for some time now, Dmitry,
but I thought a resolution may appear
by itself.

          (Dmitry's mouth is half full of
          sandwich.)

DMITRY

What is that?

                    YURI
I have been needing the little boys
room for some time now, but ship has
proved to be a bit elusive in that
department. I should have gone at
airport.

                   DMITRY
Perhaps, we both should have. It will
become quite unpleasant in here, and I
fear we will spoil the room's aesthetic
quality.

          (At that moment, a cubicle 3
          feet x 3 feet slides out of the
          wall. Dmitry looks inside. A
          bowl that looks like a toilet
          is in the centre of the cubicle
          and 3 green crystals float in
          the air about 4 feet above the
          bowl.)

                   DMITRY
Yuri look, a water closet. Somebody is
definitely listening to us.

          (Yuri gets up and looks
          inside.)

                    YURI
That is incredible, there was nothing
there, not even line in wall. Now
look, it is toilet. I wonder what
those green crystals are for?   It is
quite remarkable how they are just
hanging there. Well, if you don't

mind, I will take off my space suit and
make use of facilities.

> (Dmitry and Yuri take care of
> business and return to their
> beds dressed in their standard
> grey boiler suit.)

DMITRY

Do you have any chocolate Yuri? I need
a sugar fix.

YURI

I have an apple, if that will do?

DMITRY

Yes, that will be fine.

YURI

Quite remarkable those green crystals,
I feel lovely and clean all over and I
even smell quite fragrant.

DMITRY

Yes, it was quite an unusual
experience, but it is always nice to be
clean. I must say, I even feel
rejuvenated. If we weren't stuck in
this room we could get going.

> (The water closet retracts into
> the wall. There is no sign it
> ever existed. Yuri rises from
> his bed and walks over to the
> wall opposite the beds.)

                    YURI
Maybe there is a way out, maybe all we
have to do is ask for it.

                    DMITRY
You might be onto something there...

        (Dmitry gets up from his bed
        and stands next to Yuri.)

...Door. ...Open door. ...Exit, what
else?

                    YURI
Maybe it is more of a generalisation
than a command. Try a different
sentence structure. When the water
closet came out we were just hinting at
something we would like to do, it was
more suggestive than direct.

                    DMITRY
I think someone is pulling our strings
Yuri, and they did not want mess that's
all.

                    YURI
Maybe... 'I would like to leave now.'

        (A seam appears in the wall in
        front of them and the wall
        disappears.)

                    DMITRY
Yuri, you have done it. Quick grab our
stuff and let's get out of here.

*(Yuri and Dmitry put their
space suits back on and collect
the remaining food and supplies
they have left and leave the
white room.)*

Scene fades.

ACT 4, SCENE 2

Now faced with an exit out of the white
room, Dmitry and Yuri walk forward into
the unknown. They can see a circle of
orange seats.

                    DMITRY
We are still here. We haven't gone
anywhere, we are still in airport
terminal.

          (The doorway behind them
          returns to a wall. Yuri runs
          his hand along the wall.)

                    YURI
The wall is solid again. It is magic.
It is best illusion I have seen since
my great uncle Gonzofsky performed his
'Card-in-Fish' trick for my friends and
I on my seventh birthday.

                    DMITRY
This place is nuts, can't get my head
around it...

          (Dmitry looks around the
          airport trying to grasp the
          situation.)

...sorry, what did you say?

                    YURI
I was telling you about my great uncle

Gonzofsky.

                    DMITRY
Did he own a magic show?

                    YURI
No, he just performed for the
neighbourhood kids for birthdays and
special events.

        (Dmitry looks bewildered.)

                    DMITRY
Did he have an invisible wall trick?

                    YURI
No, nothing like that. My great uncle
Gonzofsky did a trick with a goose egg,
some hair clips and paper bag.
Sometimes he would get it right and
amaze my friends, other times he would
get real egg mixed up with fake one.
When that happened the egg would break
in bag and go all over his face and
jacket. Either way, we all enjoyed the
act. The rest of show involved making
dogs from balloons and bending spoons.
For his final trick he would invite a
member of the audience, usually one of
my friends, to come and stand next to
him. He would ask them to pick a card
and sign it. After that he would burn
card in ashtray. He would then go to
my mother's fridge, cut open a fish,
and card would be inside with my
friend's signature on it.

DMITRY
Sounds unbelievable...

(Dmitry is scratching his head
and looking everywhere.)

...Card in fish. Fantastic!

(Yuri takes out his little
tartan bear and takes out a
cigarette, lights it and begins
to smoke.)

YURI
After a few birthday parties, my mother
started to complain about waste of
fish, so my great uncle Gonzofsky
thought he would get card from my
mother's brassiere instead of fish in
fridge. Unfortunately his hand got
stuck trying to retrieve it and a fight
broke out between him and my father.
My friends thought this was part of
show and found it hilarious. Then my
father grabbed my uncle's arm, and
chocolate coins, goldfish, rabbits,
handkerchiefs, and white doves came
flying out into room. All of my
friends started to clap and my mother
and father, along with my great uncle,
all ended up outside in garden pool.
He was never invited back again. So I
never did find out truth about 'Card-
in-Fish' trick.

(Dmitry looks around one more
time.)

                    DMITRY
C'mon, let's get going. Whatever
happens let's try and stay awake, I
don't want to be locked in white cell
again...

          (Dmitry and Yuri head further
          into the airport and come to a
          brown door at the end of the
          terminal.)

Let's try this one, it might lead us
out of here.

          (Yuri takes a long puff on his
          cigarette and then puts it
          out.)

                    YURI
It's your call.

          (Yuri and Dmitry walk through
          the door and see a white room
          with white squares on the
          floor. In the centre of the
          squares is a turquoise circle
          with tiny lights of blue and
          green. On the other side of
          the room is another door.)

                    DMITRY
Look, there is another door, let's try
it.

                    YURI
Okay.

*(The door behind them closes
and disappears. The door in
front of them also disappears.
They are now stuck in the
room.)*

DMITRY
No, not again. I don't believe it!

*(At that moment a man with a
rather large handlebar
moustache, dressed in a tuxedo
and top hat, appears in the
centre of the room floating
above the turquoise circle.)*

MOUSTACHIOED MAN
Step on the square to start the game.

*(Yuri and Dmitry look on
bewildered. The man appears to
be translucent.)*

YURI
He is not real Dmitry, he is hologram.

DMITRY
What game? I am confused, what shall
we do?

MOUSTACHIOED MAN
*Step on the square to start the
game...*

(Yuri and Dmitry look at each

*other in silence as the
moustachioed man folds his arms
and looks cross.)*

MOUSTACHIOED MAN
...Please start. To begin, select a
square and simply walk onto it.

YURI
I think you should stand on a square
Dmitry.

*(Dmitry walks forward and
stands on a square, it turns
green and a bell is heard. The
Moustachioed man disappears and
what looks like an opponent
appears in front of the squares
on the opposite side. It is a
dark figure wearing a hooded
cloak carrying a scythe - it
looks like a close cousin of
the grim reaper. It takes a
step onto a square and it turns
green. A bell is heard.)*

DMITRY
The next time, you step on square. I
have harvester of death as opponent. I
hope this is not real game for soul.

YURI
I think it is your turn Dmitry.

*(Dmitry walks forward and the
square turns orange. A higher*

*tone is heard this time. The
black figure walks onto another
square and it turns green. A
bell rings.)*

                DMITRY
I think I will go diagonally this time.

        *(Dmitry steps diagonally onto
        another square and it turns
        red. A siren is heard. The
        black figure moves forward in
        front of Dmitry and swings its
        scythe. Dmitry ducks and the
        figure disappears. The
        Moustachioed man reappears in
        the centre of the board.)*

            MUSTACHIOED MAN
Sorry, you stepped on a red square,
your game is over.   ...Please say,
'Play Again.' or simply wait for your
exit to appear. Better luck next time.

        (The two doors reappear.)

                DMITRY
Yuri, the door. It is back. Let's get
out of here.

        *(They leave through the door
        they came in by and make their
        way back to the circle of
        orange seats.)*

                    YURI
This place is madhouse, we must be dead
Dmitry. That's it, we are dead! Our
bodies are still floating in black
vacuum outside of *Space Station*, and we
are dead. What was that stupid square
room all about? It seemed pointless
and absurd. ...And hologram with
moustache, what purpose does he serve
on ship?

                    DMITRY
Look Yuri, the blank signs we saw
earlier all have writing now... 'CHECK
IN HERE' ...'TERMINAL 1' ...
'ARRIVALS' ...'DEPARTURES' ...
'INFORMATION' ... 'BAGGAGE'
...'TOILETS' ...'SHOPS' ...'EXIT TO
UPPER DECKS' Look! Look above where
we were trapped in white room –
'GOLIATH GALACTIC STAR CRUISES, waiting
and wash Room.'

                    YURI
Goliath Galactic Star Cruises?

          (*Dmitry runs around the airport
          terminal shouting.*)

                    DMITRY
I get it, I get it, I understand.

          (*He returns back to Yuri, who
          is now sitting down on the
          orange seats smoking a
          cigarette.*)

                    YURI

Get what? We are finished Dmitry.
This place is crazy, it is asylum for
insane and we are latest guests. I
think this ship is laughing at us; it
is obviously organic space entity who
is playing mind games with us before it
digests us in its stomach.

                   DMITRY

I never thought of that. No Yuri,
don't you see. It is a cruise ship for
outer space.

     (Yuri takes a drag from his
     cigarette.)

                    YURI

What?

                   DMITRY

It's just a cruise ship for universe.
Think about it Yuri, big storage areas
with boxes and crates, decorative
designs in lifts, a terminal for
departing and arriving passengers and a
waiting room for weary travellers - not
a prison, like we first thought, but
waiting room!

                    YURI

Waiting room? What about valves and
turret monster with pulse weapon and
the banks of reel to reel tape
machines? It's nuts.

152

                    DMITRY
Yuri, use your imagination. Think of
life as big brush with enormous canvas
to paint on?

                     YURI
I tried using my imagination in art
class once and my teacher, Mrs.
Karkrashnia, wrote report back to my
parents.

                    DMITRY
What did she say?

                     YURI
I remember it well... 'Yuri shows very
little interest in his art class and is
completely inept with a paint brush.
He shows a general lack of aptitude for
creativity and has little to no
imagination when approaching the
simplest of tasks, in fact, I have seen
monkeys at the zoo create superior
works of art by walking over a canvas
in their bare feet.'...

                    DMITRY
What did your parents say?

                     YURI
They did not take news well, especially
my father. He crept out later that
night and cut brake pipes to teacher's
car.

                    DMITRY
What? What happened to teacher?

                    YURI
She drove car to go to school in
morning and crashed into group of nuns
on way to abbey.

                    DMITRY
Was anyone injured?

                    YURI
No, but teacher was charged with
reckless endangerment and lost her
licence.

                    DMITRY
That is terrible Dmitry.

                    YURI
Not so bad, there was no more art
classes for rest of semester.

     (Dmitry stares at Yuri,
     scratches his head for a while
     and rubs his chin.)

                    DMITRY
Okay, forget about what I said. Valves
were probably consignment for planet in
early stages of electronics.

                    YURI
But I thought you said this was cruise
ship?

DMITRY

It is, but it also probably traded with
other worlds along route. You are
bound to need fresh food, alcohol and
clothing. Maybe valve is like coin on
some planets.

YURI

Don't forget cigarettes Dmitry, they
are most important freight for any long
journey.

DMITRY

Yes, cloud of smoke and stale air are
always welcome guest!

YURI

So, why is ship here?

DMITRY

I don't know... but let's say, you are
cruise ship that travels the cosmos,
offering new and exciting destinations
to your customers. Now, let's say you
discover Earth and send down a survey
team to investigate planet's
suitability. At first, everything
seems fine, the planet appears to be
safe destination for guests and
everyone is having good time, except
after a few weeks, some visitors start
to feel sick, and some even die. What
does the captain do?

YURI

You are asking me, I am still trying to

figure out room with squares...

> (*Yuri takes a drink from the*
> *bottle of water.*)

...I guess, I guess I would quarantine those infected, get everyone off planet and contact home world to tell them of problem.

YURI

DMITRY
Exactly. That's what I would do if I was captain of big galactic cruise ship...

> (*Dmitry fastens a loose pocket*
> *on his trouser leg and*
> *continues.*)

...At some point, sickness spreads throughout whole of ship. Now, this is bigger problem for home world. After they learn that Earth is destroyer of immortality, they send military force to erect Dome to seal off aberrant planet from rest of universe. The ship is left behind to power Dome, and weaponry, like that turret monster in cargo bay area, is kept on board to protect ship from pillagers. They leave a small crew for Dome maintenance, and return home.

YURI
But what about crew, where are they now?

                    DMITRY
Maybe they are dead, it has been 5,000
years. A lot can happen in that time.

                    YURI
It is plausible explanation... Better
than alien entity that wants to eat us.
I prefer your exposition to mine... and
I am happy to retract my assessment of
the situation... and therefore, propose
we move forward on the assumption that
your hypothesis is correct...

      (Yuri takes a sip of water.)

...Which way should we go now?

                    DMITRY
Well, we have sign saying, 'EXIT TO
UPPER DECKS', so I suggest we go that
way...

      (Yuri replaces the bottle of
      water into his space suit and
      stands up. They make their way
      to the exit door.)

... The door seems stuck!

                    YURI
Give it a push.

                    DMITRY
What do you think I am doing? It is no
good, it is stuck solid.

                    YURI
Let me try.

                    DMITRY
Be my guest.

          *(Yuri walks passed Dmitry to
          the door, pulls it towards him
          and it opens immediately.)*

                    YURI
Ah, that is it. After you...

          *(Dmitry looks at Yuri with
          annoyance and walks through the
          door. He is now looking at a
          vast amount of steps leading
          upwards. Yuri has not moved
          from his spot.)*

...What do you see?

          (Dmitry looks back at Yuri.)

                    DMITRY
Why are you still over there?

                    YURI
I do not trust door, at moment I do not
trust my senses.

                    DMITRY
It is alright. It is stairwell. There
are a lot of steps going upwards, but
that is where ship's bridge is, so it
is good omen.

(Yuri walks through the door.)

                    YURI
A lot of steps you say, that will take
hours to get to top.

                   DMITRY
Maybe not hours, but a good while.

Scene fades.

ACT 4, SCENE 3

Dmitry and Yuri enter the stairwell. It is of a concrete design with a metal handrail. The walls are grey and tiny oval lights spiral up the staircase like lights on a Christmas tree. After 30 minutes, Yuri is ready for a rest.

                    YURI
Dmitry, I am ready for a rest, my lungs are on fire.

                  DMITRY
Just a little longer, I see gap up ahead.

          *(Yuri is puffing and holding
          his chest. He stops for a
          second and looks up.)*

                    YURI
Dmitry, do you see what I see?

                  DMITRY
That depends, what do you see?

          (Yuri is still looking up.)

                    YURI
That gap you spoke of.

                  DMITRY
What about it?

                    YURI
It is missing staircase, about 60
feet's worth.

        (Dmitry looks up and sees there
        is a huge gap. He is still
        walking, but Yuri has stopped.)

                  DMITRY
You are right, I will go a little
further and see how bad it is...

        (Dmitry arrives at the gap.
        There is no way up, but a door
        is accessible before the gap.
        He shouts down to Yuri.)

...There is door up here, maybe we can
get out.

                    YURI
Try it before I come up, see if it
opens.

        (Yuri sits on a step and lights
        a cigarette. Dmitry pushes the
        door and it opens.)

                  DMITRY
It is alright. We can get out this
way.

        (Yuri walks up the stairs,
        still puffing on his cigarette
        and pushes the door open.
        Dmitry is waiting on the other

*side pressing some buttons on a
lift that is situated in a long
corridor.)*

                    DMITRY

Good.   You are here.   What took you so
long?

                    YURI

I stopped for chocolate Éclair at
French pastry shop just before exit
door.   I would have got you one but I
had no more valves to trade.

(Dmitry looks at Yuri.)

                    DMITRY

That is Okay, I prefer Mille-feuille.

(They both laugh.)

                    YURI

What are you doing now?

                    DMITRY

Seeing if lift works, but there is no
power.

                    YURI

I will help you push door open...

*(Yuri and Dmitry push and pull
at the door for a while; it
begins to move slowly upwards,
making a terrible scraping*

*sound.   It opens all the way
and they can see inside.   On
the floor lies a figure, it is
the skeleton of an alien,
dressed in a tattered blue and
red uniform.)*

... What is that?

DMITRY
It looks like the ship's captain.

YURI
How can you tell it is captain?

*(Dmitry and Yuri walk into the
lift and crouch down by the
figure.)*

DMITRY
Look at his shoulder epaulettes, there
are four pips on each side, so he is
captain of ship. I have not seen that
type of insignia before, but four
icons, in this case 'Golden Moths',
usually means captain, unless different
planets in cosmos have disparate way to
indicate military rank.

*(Yuri looks at the golden
objects and touches them.)*

YURI
I do not think they are moths; the
wings are on bottom, more like plane
than moth. Perhaps he is high ranking

janitor or fashion coordinator for rich
guests...

>   (*Yuri starts to examine the
>   skull.*)

...Look at skull Dmitry, the eye
sockets are huge, definitely not human.

DMITRY
No, look at his hands, just three
fingers and a thumb.

>   (*Yuri rubs his right hand over
>   the skeletons skull and
>   examines it closely.*)

YURI
Here is proof it is not human, there is
only one parietal plate and skull is
quite elongated, definitely
extraterrestrial in origin. There is
big hole in occipital bone in back of
skull, must have been cause of death...

>   (*Dmitry picks up a silver
>   coloured metal bar with a brown
>   stained end with a few strands
>   of stray fibres on the tip and
>   begins poking a metal case on
>   the floor.*)

...probably a blunt instrument, like a
heavy bar of some kind.

>   (*Dmitry stares at the end of
>   the bar in his hand and Yuri*)

*begins rifling through the
pockets of the corpse and finds
a gold medallion encrusted with
diamonds, emeralds, sapphires
and amethyst stones.)*

DMITRY
Would you say bar was three feet long
with a flat end?

*(Yuri discreetly puts the
medallion in his pocket and
continues searching the body.)*

YURI
Yes, that sounds about right, quite a
solid bar I would say.

*(Dmitry throws the bar on the
floor. When the bar hits the
floor, the lift begins to move
slightly and groan.)*

YURI
What are you doing?

DMITRY
Quick, let's get out of here...

*(Dmitry bends down and grabs
the metal case and exits the
lift. Yuri is knocked off
balance and falls to the floor.
The lift starts to move and
shake. Scraping and grinding
noises reverberate in the lift*

*and the sound of cables
snapping and cracking can be
heard.)*

...Hurry Yuri, it is falling.

*(Yuri gets to his feet and
jumps out of the lift. On his
exit the lift breaks free and
begins falling. Cables lashing
and metal grinding can be
heard.   The lift door
closes... Silence.)*

YURI
Why did you throw heavy bar on floor?
You nearly killed us.

DMITRY
Sorry Yuri, I realised I was holding
murder weapon of our alien cousin and I
had put my finger prints on it - I am
now likely suspect in interstellar
incident.

YURI
What! Are you crazy? That body has
been lying there for hundreds of years;
it was dead before you were even born.

DMITRY
That is big relief, I thought *Cosmic
Police* would track me down and keep me
in suspended animation for a thousand
years as punishment.

166

                    YURI
You should be so lucky.

                    DMITRY
You are right, with my luck I would be
put in front of big T.V. where they
only show amateur wrestling to music of
Stravinsky.

        *(Yuri notices the metal case
        Dmitry is holding.)*

                    YURI
What do you have there?

                    DMITRY
Oh, this...

        (Dmitry lifts up the case.)

...it is case, I think it might be
flight case for captain. It might have
star charts and ship's schematics,
maybe even clue for getting off ship.

                    YURI
That would be good, let's open it.

        *(Dmitry and Yuri look at the
        closed case.)*

                    DMITRY
I think we will need to find something
to pry it open with.

                    YURI
A pity you threw away bar...

     *(Yuri looks around the
     corridor.)*

...I will check down here.

     *(Yuri walks down the corridor
     and sees lots of doors with
     symbols on them. He pushes a
     door open and looks in.)*

                    YURI
Dmitry, come here. We have window. I
can see Earth.

     *(Dmitry walks over to Yuri, and
     they walk into the room.)*

                    DMITRY
We are in cabin.

                    YURI
This is more like suite. I am not a
big fan of white, but it is very
spacious and view is terrific.

     *(They walk over to a group of
     windows that span the length of
     the suite.)*

                    DMITRY
I was beginning to think we would never
see Earth again. It looks beautiful
from this high up.

*(Yuri takes out a cigarette and
begins to smoke. He moves
closer to Dmitry and puts his
hand on his shoulder.)*

                    YURI
It is pleasing sight, even if it is
flat like empty envelope.

                    DMITRY
It is home Yuri, who cares about shape.
Maybe if others could see it from up
here, they would not be so worried
about planet's secret...

    *(Dmitry places the metal case
    on the floor.)*

...What a shame we did not bring
camera.

                    YURI
I have camera in pocket.

                    DMITRY
I did not even consider taking it, why
did you?

                    YURI
I thought we might need to leave
message for posterity, just in case we
did not escape ship and get back home.

                    DMITRY
Give it to me. I want to film Earth

from window. If we do get back, we
will show world and tell truth for
once.

                    YURI
Here, take camera. I am going to rest
feet for a while.

          (Yuri passes Dmitry the video
          camera, then walks over to a
          large sofa in the middle of the
          suite. He sits down and starts
          to eat some sausage.)

                    YURI
It is good to have seat. Would you
like some sausage Dmitry?

          (Dmitry is holding the camera
          and filming out the window. He
          turns to face Yuri.)

                    DMITRY
I am alright just now, that turkey and
cranberry sandwich I had earlier keeps
repeating on me, there must have been a
strange spice within the stuffing mix
that I am not used to...

          (Dmitry turns off the video
          camera and rubs his stomach.
          He turns to face Yuri.)

...But a little whisky would settle it
down I am sure.

                    YURI
I guess you have earned a drink, but I
will keep bottle, this is the last of
it and who knows if we will ever get
out of this place.

          (Yuri pours some whisky into
          the bottle lid and passes it to
          Dmitry. Dmitry hands back the
          video camera.)

                   DMITRY
Thank you Yuri...

          (Dmitry drinks down the whisky
          and hands back the lid to
          Yuri.)

...I think we should rest up for a
while. Perhaps after a little sleep,
we can try opening that case to see
what's inside.

                    YURI
That suits me fine, I am quite
comfortable here and the view is quite
soporific.

Scene fades.

ACT 4, SCENE 4

A couple of hours have passed and Yuri is fast asleep on the sofa. Dmitry is removing an air vent cover with a screwdriver.

YURI

What is noise?

DMITRY

Yuri, I think I have found a way out.

YURI

Good, but it is shame that you were not a little slower, I was about to be served a nice Lobster Chowder, then I heard a banging and waiter dropped dish on floor.

> *(Dmitry removes an air vent cover and a cool breeze blows through the vent into the room.)*

DMITRY

Yuri, smell that air, it is so fresh, it will wake you up.

> *(Dmitry sticks his head in the vent and then looks back at the sofa, but Yuri is now standing over him with a cigarette in his hand.)*

                    YURI
So, this is way out?

          (Yuri pokes his head in the
          vent and blows smoke.)

                    DMITRY
Yes, the ship's schematics show shaft
leading to bridge.

                    YURI
Where did you get schematics for ship?

                    DMITRY
From case.

                    YURI
How did you open it?

                    DMITRY
I would like to tell you that it was
very difficult, but the truth is, I
dropped it and it fell open.

                    YURI
Lucky break for us. Was there anything
else inside?

                    DMITRY
Just a scroll of blank paper.

          (Yuri walks over to the case
          and picks up the scroll. He
          unrolls it and holds it up to
          the light. Symbols and images

*start to appear on the blank
paper.)*

YURI
Look at this Dmitry, this paper is
showing something, images and symbols
are appearing. They are dancing over
page like ballerina on ice. Strange
letters, icons.

*(Dmitry walks over to see the
scroll. A small musical trill
is heard and the images remain
static.)*

DMITRY
What do you think it is?

YURI
If I did not know better, I would say
it is futuristic computer. If we were
at home, we could sell this for big
truck of Rubles.

DMITRY
Computer?

(Dmitry looks at the page.)

...What language is that?

YURI
Your guess is as good as mine.

*(Yuri and Dmitry look at the
page and the language changes*

to English.)

DMITRY
Look! It has changed to English. Must
be like blank signs in airport. Press
on that icon there Yuri that says
'LOG'.

*(Yuri presses on the icon and a
figure with a large head, big
eyes, wearing a blue and red
uniform appears and starts to
talk. It is a video log by the
deceased captain.)*

DECEASED CAPTAIN
*...Day 526 in space. Most of the crew
have been poisoned. At first we
thought a crew member had returned from
the planet's surface with a harmful
organism, a strange mushroom or fungus
that hadn't been detected by the ship's
bio scans. A virus seemed to be the
logical conclusion, but after
exhausting every known disease and
listing the patients' symptoms, we
started to look at other causes. It was
Commander LÁ-Ever that discovered the
truth behind the outbreak. SAL, our
head of security, had been poisoning
the ship's water supply with EgÁvol - a
deadly plant from the LisÁb quadrant.
Unfortunately, we discovered the truth
too late, the effects of this poison
are irreversible. Why SAL decided on
this course of action is unclear.
After running several diagnostic tests,*

*Commander LÁ-Ever discovered missing
entries and anomalies within her
programme, whether this was self-
inflicted or the actions of a another
party is still to be determined.
Before Commander LÁ-Ever could finish
his investigation, he was found dead
along with crewman Énog. They had been
bludgeoned to death by a long metal
bar. Tomorrow, some of the crew are
returning to the surface with SAL in
the guise of searching for a vaccine.
Hopefully she can be overpowered or
left on the planet. On EgÁs, they are
preparing for our arrival in 3 days
time...*

(The page goes blank.)

                    DMITRY
What happened?

                    YURI
It just went back to paper. At least
it worked long enough to give us an
indication of what happened on ship.

(Yuri looks at Dmitry.)

                    DMITRY
It seemed they were all killed by head
of security, but what was all that talk
about her programme?

                    YURI
She must be artificial lifeform, like

advanced robot or something.

                    DMITRY
Robot in charge of security, what a
joke. If you make robot head of
security, you are bound to have
problems. I can't even get my electric
can opener to work on a regular basis.

                     YURI
I know what you mean, my electric
cheese grater only works if you cut
cheese into thin strips before you feed
it, then you have to make sure cheese
is 4 degrees Celsius before it will
work.

                    DMITRY
You have an electric cheese grater?

                     YURI
Yeh, sure. The wife was complaining
about damaging her nails, so I bought
her one for Christmas present 3 years
ago.

                    DMITRY
I would have liked to have seen look on
her face Christmas morning.

                     YURI
I know, it was best model on market.
Perhaps, that was problem with robot,
maybe they just bought a cheap second-
hand unit from a disreputable

dealership.

                    DMITRY
That may have happened, who am I to say
any different. In any case, that SAL
sounds like a psychopath, a real cold
blooded killer with no morals or
empathy for others, I am glad she is
dead...

          (*Dmitry looks across to the
          vent and straightens his space
          suit.*)

...I think we better get going. Take
the scroll just in case it comes back
to life.

                    YURI
Okay.

          (*Yuri places the scroll in his
          pocket.*)

                    DMITRY
Y'know, my stomach is still giving me
trouble, I don't think I will eat for a
while.

                    YURI
Good, because there is no more food.
We have a few sips of water and some
whisky.

                    DMITRY
What happened to sausage?

                    YURI
I ate it!

                    DMITRY
You didn't save me any?

                    YURI
You had upset stomach. It is better to
fast for a few days when your stomach
is poorly.

                    DMITRY
I guess I will have to put your advice
into practice. C'mon, let's get out of
here.

          *(Yuri and Dmitry enter the
          shaft and start to climb
          upwards on a recessed step that
          is part of the interior.
          Dmitry is in front.)*

                    YURI
Can you see anything yet?

                    DMITRY
Yes, it has come to a stop and there is
another vent leading into a room.

                    YURI
Can you get out?

                    DMITRY
I will give it a kick.

*(Dmitry kicks the vent and it
falls to the floor in the room.
From his view point, he can see
the room is full of cogs and
gears. A small metal step
leads down from the vent to the
floor. He climbs out and
enters the room. Yuri follows
shortly after.)*

YURI

Look at this place, it's like the
inside of a grandfather clock. The
cogs are huge, look at that spring, it
must be 15 feet in diameter.

*(Dmitry and Yuri walk into the
room.)*

DMITRY

Look at that gearing mechanism and that
big flywheel, it's the size of a
fairground ride. Everything looks like
it was made in Victorian era, brass
cogs and steel pulleys. It's
fantastic, unbelievable.

*(Yuri and Dmitry walk further
into the room and look at
everything in wonderment.
Slightly above them, up a small
staircase, is an enormous brass
plinth supporting some sort of
control station.)*

180

                    YURI
Look there Dmitry, that might be
something.

          (Dmitry and Yuri make their way
          up the small staircase and onto
          the plinth. In front of them
          are hundreds of levers and
          handles, circular knobs,
          buttons, coloured lights,
          instrument gauges and graph
          readouts, temperature
          indicators, volume controls,
          capacity and speed indicators,
          dials, voltage meters and
          displays filled with blue and
          green liquids.)

                    DMITRY
What do you make of all this Yuri?

                    YURI
Don't you know? It is popcorn machine!

          (Yuri looks at a dial with
          florescent green liquid
          inside.)

                    DMITRY
What do you think this does?

                    YURI
It is fluoride regulator for
toothpaste.

          (Dmitry looks at a display

*flashing a cog and spring
symbol.)*

DMITRY
Yuri, look at this one with the
flashing cog and spring, what does that
do?

YURI
You mean you honestly don't know? It
is hyper drive button engaging gear for
travelling at speeds faster than light.

(They both laugh.)

DMITRY
I am almost tempted to press buttons
and pull levers, it looks a lot of fun.

*(They study the overwhelming
array of buttons and dials for
a while and then turn around to
face two mammoth gold doors.)*

YURI
Dmitry, that is impressive. Did you
ever see a pair of doors as spectacular
as those.

DMITRY
They are quite awe inspiring, what do
you think is inside?

YURI
Let's see...

               (Yuri walks up to the doors,
               they are closed tightly. In
               the centre about 3 feet from
               the ground there is a circular
               indentation that looks like a
               locking mechanism.)

...I don't think we are getting in here
in a hurry.

                    DMITRY
I bet the bridge is behind that door,
let me see...

               (Dmitry pokes at the lock with
               his finger.)

...This is very specialised lock Yuri,
looks like it needs a circular key with
different shaped extrusions. I think
we will have to find another way in...

               (Yuri reaches into his top
               pocket to grab a cigarette and
               pulls out the alien captain's
               medallion at the same time.
               The medallion falls to the
               floor and rolls towards
               Dmitry's feet. Dmitry bends
               down and picks it up.)

...What is this?

                    YURI
I don't know, I found it on alien
captain when I went through his
pockets.

                    DMITRY
It looks like gold, with diamonds,
emeralds, sapphires, and these look
like amethysts, it must be worth a
small fortune...

          (Dmitry looks at the medallion
          in awe, then looks up at Yuri.)

...When were you going to tell me about
it?

                    YURI
What do you mean?

                    DMITRY
What do I mean? You find gold relic
with precious jewels and conveniently
forget to mention it.

                    YURI
It isn't like that Dmitry, we have been
preoccupied with escaping ship and I
simply forgot about trinket, that is
all.

                    DMITRY
You were going to keep treasure for
yourself. I see now how you have
amassed fortune from family members.
You are rat Yuri, a snake in grass,
just like your chicken stealing father
- a liar with a smile, a dirty scheming
villain who befriends people for
purpose of gain.

(Yuri looks shocked.)

                    YURI
Dmitry, I think you are under spell.
Why would I keep trinket for self, I
just forgot, that is all. I nearly
fell to my death in lift, and then, had
to console you immediately afterwards
over fingerprint concerns. I have
given you half of everything I have had
on trip: whisky, vodka, sausages,
bread, stew - I even gave you half of
my oxygen when ship was falling apart.
I don't know how you can say such
things.

        *(Dmitry thinks about Yuri's
        words for a moment and looks
        him in the face.)*

                    DMITRY
You are right Yuri, you have been a
good friend, it must be this place, I
am anxious to get on Bridge. Please
forget what I said.

        *(Yuri looks across at Dmitry
        and notices the similarity
        between the medallion in his
        hand and the lock on the Bridge
        door.)*

                    YURI
Dmitry, the trinket, look at lock on
door, it is similar in shape.

(Dmitry holds the medallion in front of the lock. The medallion is smaller and has an extra side but fits in the hole. Dmitry wedges the medallion in the door and the lock turns. After a few clunking sounds the doors begin to open.)

                    DMITRY
Yuri, we've done it, it is Bridge of ship. Look, there is Earth. Just look at the size of this ship from up here, it's crazy...

(Dmitry looks back at Yuri, and Yuri looks on amazed. Dmitry starts to walk onto the Bridge.)

...Did you ever see a Bridge space as stupendous as this, it's ridiculous!

(Yuri joins Dmitry on the Bridge. The room is 100 feet long and 50 feet wide. A single window runs the entire length of the Bridge to give a fantastic panoramic view of Earth. Everywhere is white and clean. In the centre of the Bridge sits a holographic representation of Earth covered by the Dome. There are no other panels or controls. Dmitry and Yuri walk over to

the holographic display.)

YURI

Look there, a hologram of Earth with
Dome. What is that strange fluctuation
of colour to Dome barrier?

DMITRY

Must be showing areas of weakness in
force field. Look at that red bar
moving up and down, must be power
failure. There are quite a few holes
in field, looks like it is failing.

YURI

How do we turn it off, there are no
controls in this room?

(A voice is heard behind them,
and they turn around to see who
is there. In front of them is
a woman with pure white skin,
red eyes and red hair, wearing
a ruched sleeved jumpsuit and
Jazz shoes. Her clothes are
oily and dirty and look worn.
There are several powder burns
on her abdomen and a thick
black scar is visible on her
neck.)

MYSTERY WOMAN

You can't turn it off. Why would you
want to?

                    DMITRY
To save planet...

        (Dmitry looks at Yuri then back
        at the woman.)

...We didn't think anyone was on board,
we thought crew was dead.

                MYSTERY WOMAN
They are.

                    DMITRY
Then, if you don't mind me asking, who
are you?

        (The woman walks closer.)

                MYSTERY WOMAN
I'm SAL.

                     YURI
Did you say Sal?

        (Yuri looks at Dmitry with
        concern.)

                MYSTERY WOMAN
Sentient. Artificial. Lifeform. SAL
for short.

                    DMITRY
Then you are not real, you are robot?

                    SAL
That depends on what you mean by real.
I have a physical shape and form, and I
can comprehend my existence. I am as
real as you are.

                    YURI
How long have you been here?

                    SAL
A long time, since the virus outbreak
on Earth, some 5,000 years ago.

        (Dmitry and Yuri look on at the
        woman with a touch of
        uneasiness. SAL's voice,
        although soft and controlled,
        has an underlying note of
        intimidation.)

                  DMITRY
SAL, if I may be permitted another
question?...

        (SAL nods.)

...What is your purpose here?

                    SAL
I am the head of security, my purpose
here is to protect the ship, to
maintain the containment field you call
the Dome - at all costs.

                  DMITRY
I see. So you were left here by

yourself to carry out this task?

                    SAL
No, there were others.

                    DMITRY
What happened to them?

                    SAL
Why are you asking these questions?

        (Dmitry looks at Yuri for
        inspiration.)

                    YURI
Erm, ...We are an independent retrieval
agency sent here to collect outstanding
back taxes in the amount of five
thousand Rubles from a Mr.
Rumpelstiltskinov, do you know of his
whereabouts?

                    SAL
Rumpelstiltskinov? There has never
been anyone here with that name...

        (SAL's head turns sideways.)

...checking database ...checking. No,
there has never been a crew member here
with that name.

                    YURI
Sorry to have troubled you, we must
have been misinformed...

*(Dmitry looks at Yuri and
raises his eyebrows. Yuri
faces SAL again.)*

...I think we have taken up enough of
your time, we won't trouble you any
further. If you will excuse us, we
will be on our way. It was obviously a
clerical error. Thank you for your
help.

*(Dmitry and Yuri start to walk
towards the big doors, but they
start to close.)*

SAL
Where do you think you are going?

*(Dmitry and Yuri turn back
around and face SAL.*

DMITRY
We have important meeting with CEO of
Russian Meat Emporium, to discuss his
Capital Gains Allowance for the last
year. If we do not hurry, I feel we
will be late.

SAL
You cannot leave, it is impossible.
How you have managed to get this far, I
do not know. No one leaves this ship,
the crew wanted to leave, but I had to
stop them. They wanted to go down to
that planet with its infectious

inhabitants...

> (*SAL points at Earth through
> the window. Upon raising her
> arm her top rips at the
> shoulder.*)

...They said they had cured the disease
and it was safe, but how could I trust
them, they would have said anything to
get off this ship.

(*Dmitry looks at Yuri.*)

                    DMITRY
How could they do that?

                    SAL
By shuttle of course.

                    DMITRY
Sorry, I meant to say, why would they
do that?

                    SAL
Enough. Now tell me, where is your
ship?

                    YURI
Our ship?

                    SAL
Yes, your ship. My sensors did not
alert me of a vessel. Where is it?

192

YURI

It was des...

     (Dmitry interrupts Yuri, and walks in front of him.)

DMITRY

...It is parked off the starboard bow.

     (SAL looks out the window.)

SAL

Where? I do not see it.

YURI

It is... It is cloaked!

SAL

Cloaked? What do you mean?

DMITRY

It is invisible.

SAL

Invisible? That's impossible!

YURI

Not really, it is just clever technology.

     (SAL continues to look out of the window. She seems to be running some sort of algorithm in her brain. She is quite still, but her head is moving.)

She begins to pace the room.)

SAL
Earlier, when we first met, you said you wanted to save the planet. That is your true purpose here. That means you want to destroy this ship?

YURI
No, that was not intention. We were sent from Earth as emissary to make first contact with entity on black ship...

(Yuri moves closer to SAL with his arms open.)

...We had no knowledge of your existence.

SAL
You lie. No one can get through the protective barrier.

(Yuri looks at Dmitry.)

DMITRY
Then how do you explain us?

SAL
...Processing. ...Processing. Incorrect inquiry. Subroutine failure... Insufficient data...

(Dmitry and Yuri look on at SAL, who is malfunctioning.)

                    DMITRY
Look! Stupid machine is broken. Let's
get out of here.

          (Dmitry and Yuri try to open
          the door, but it won't budge.
          SAL has finished processing an
          algorithm and now stands close
          behind them as they mutter and
          groan.)

                    SAL
What you are attempting is futile,
those doors can only be opened from the
inside by thought, and you must know
the code.

          (Yuri and Dmitry stop pushing
          at the door, straighten their
          space suits out and stand to
          face her.)

                    YURI
Then why not tell us code and we will
leave, it is nearly dinner time and I
am stickler for eating at correct hour.
My mother...

          (SAL interjects.)

                    SAL
...Enough of this foolish discourse.
...Now, tell me where your ship is and
how you plan to deactivate the
protective barrier?

*(Dmitry and Yuri look at each
other lost for words.)*

...Can't Remember, maybe this will
help.

*(Dmitry and Yuri fall to their
knees and their noses start to
bleed. They hold their heads
in agony and start to moan.)*

DMITRY
Stop! I will tell you.

*(SAL stops with her mind spell
on Yuri and Dmitry and they
fall to the floor.)*

SAL
Good. Now tell me where your ship is?

*(Dmitry glances at Yuri and
rolls his eyes, indicating to
play along with his story.)*

DMITRY
We only have small ship; that is why
you could not detect it. We bypassed
your security system at starboard side
shuttle bay and came in there.

SAL
I see. ...processing. ...waiting.
...you are telling the truth.

(Dmitry and Yuri look at each

*other with surprise. SAL walks
over to the window, then turns
to face them.)*

                    SAL
Now, tell me, how were you planning to
deactivate the protective barrier?

                    DMITRY
It is better if Yuri explains this part
of plan, he is more familiar with exact
details.

          *(SAL looks at Yuri. Yuri looks
          at Dmitry then back at SAL.)*

                    SAL
Well?

                    YURI
We were to come on board to see if
Dome, I mean protective barrier, could
be deactivated from bridge...

                    SAL
Yes. Go on...

                    YURI
If we could not find a way of turning
it off, we were to blow up ship.

                    SAL
Processing... Establishing
connection... Waiting... You are
telling the truth. Now, how were you

going to blow up ship?

                    DMITRY
Our vessel is full of explosives, we
were to place them on Bridge and
throughout ship.

                     SAL
Take me to your ship?

                    DMITRY
We can't!

                     SAL
I will punish you again if you do not
comply.

     (Yuri walks towards SAL.)

                     YURI
No, wait! It is not like that. We are
unfamiliar with your ship, and we had
to crawl through air vents and play
stupid game with moustachioed man - it
would take hours. You must know better
way.

                     SAL
Processing... command structure
rerouting... failure at Ámmaga
circuit... Processing... You are
telling the truth. Walk over there and
stand at that wall.

     (Dmitry and Yuri stand in front

*of a white wall. The wall
disappears and an exit leads
out to a long walk way.)*

                    SAL
Follow the tunnel to the end, I will be
right behind you.

          *(Dmitry and Yuri are now
          walking inside of a very long
          glass tunnel outside of the
          ship. They can see the
          vastness of the ship and the
          Earth with its protective
          barrier. SAL walks behind them
          processing information.)*

                    YURI
Dmitry, I don't think our new albino
friend is full bowl of fruit, what are
we going to do?   She...

          *(Yuri looks behind him to look
          at SAL.)*

...is mass murderer of ship's crew, she
will not think twice about killing us.

                    DMITRY
No, I don't suppose she will. I think
we are in trouble Yuri. We will just
have to play along.

                    YURI
Play along! What are we going to do
when we get to shuttle bay and she sees

there is no ship?

>   (SAL *is still running*
>   *algorithms and walking behind*
>   *them.)*

                    DMITRY
Do you still have laser gun?

                     YURI
Yes, laser gun is in boot and I also
have explosive device tucked in space
suit.

                    DMITRY
Where did you get that from?

                     YURI
While we were grabbing stuff to leave
space station, I grabbed one of bombs.

                    DMITRY
Does it still work, I thought you said
wires were chewed?

                     YURI
That is only for remote detonation, we
can set timer.

                    DMITRY
Good. Very good.   When we get to
shuttle bay, we will shoot our friend
and strap bomb to her, set timer and
leave using spare shuttle.

(*SAL is now talking to herself.
She moves closer.*)

                    YURI
You make it sound so simple. We don't
know anything about alien shuttle
craft, we don't even know what they
look like, they could be rabbit jelly
mould for all we know...

                   DMITRY
...Shh, she is coming.

                    SAL
There were others before who tried to
stop me...

        (*SAL mutters to herself,
        twitching and gesticulating as
        she walks.*)

...The Great Council of Arkanazak, they
wanted to remove the protective
barrier, they said it was destroying
your atmosphere, creating a greenhouse
effect. Other crew members said it
wasn't needed anymore, the virus that
the Overseers contracted was no longer
a threat. Those fools...

        (*Her fingers run along the side
        of the tunnel and she begins to
        smile.*)

...They are all dead now...

(Her smile changes to
frustration and anger.)

...only because, only because they
wouldn't listen to reason. I tried to
tell the council, but I grew tired of
their argument and killed them.

                    YURI
Your plan Dmitry, is looking much
better by the minute. If we have to
die today, well, we will die trying.

          (They are coming to the end of
          the walkway and a door opens
          leading into the shuttle bay.
          They all walk inside. In front
          of them are hundreds of black
          ovoid shapes floating 3 feet
          off the ground. They are 10ft
          x 8ft in size. The bay area is
          vast and endless. Directly in
          front of them lie the remains
          of former crew members
          scattered about the floor like
          trash.)

                    DMITRY
Well, at least we know what happened to
crew.

                    YURI
Dmitry, I will let you pilot the
shuttle craft, after all, you do out
rank me, the privilege should be all
yours.

                    DMITRY
If you can figure a way in, I will fly.

                     SAL
Stop talking. Now, where is your ship?

     *(Dmitry and Yuri turn to face
     her avoiding the corpses on the
     floor.)*

                    DMITRY
Can't you see it, it is that big black
one in the corner...

     (SAL looks into the distance.)

...Now Yuri!

     *(Yuri takes out the laser
     cutter from his boot and fires
     it at SAL's face. Dmitry kicks
     her in the stomach and she
     falls to the ground. Yuri
     takes out the explosive device
     and sticks it to her back. They
     run in amongst the sea of black
     shapes and hide.)*

                     YURI
What now?

                    DMITRY
See if you can get inside shuttle.

     *(Yuri looks at the black shapes
     and runs his hands along them.)*

                    YURI
How? There is no crease for door!

          (They run in amongst the shapes
          frantically looking for a way
          into the ovoid spacecraft.)

                    DMITRY
I don't know, try a command... No, a
suggestion.

          (Yuri stops at a shuttle and
          begins to speak. A voice can
          be heard in the far corner of
          the shuttle bay, it is SAL.)

                    SAL
You will die...

          (SAL is back on her feet, her
          face is badly injured and she
          looks confused and struggles to
          see.)

...You will die like all the rest.

                    YURI
Open door? ...No! Erm, I would like
to go inside please?

          (Yuri frantically waves his
          arms around then pushes and
          shoves at the shuttle, shouting
          out different commands. A few
          moments later, a high ping
          sound is heard and the black

ovoid changes shape into a sleeker, more aerodynamic design. A walkway appears leading inside the shuttle and Dmitry and Yuri enter. The walkway closes behind them and they are faced with a bright, dazzling light. Inside the shuttle it is white, nothing else, no windows or controls, just white.)

DMITRY

It is trap, there is nothing in here, it is freight carrier. Yuri, we are doomed! How long did you set timer for?

(Yuri looks around.)

YURI

5 minutes...

(Yuri looks at Dmitry.)

...maybe, just maybe. 'I WOULD LIKE A CHAIR FOR BOTH OF US.'

(Two chairs appear.)

DMITRY

It is voice activated. 'I WOULD LIKE A WINDOW TO SEE OUT.'

(A window appears.)

                    YURI
Dmitry, we must hurry. 'WE WOULD LIKE
TO LEAVE SHIP NOW.'

          *(The walkway extends and SAL
          appears at the exit.)*

                   DMITRY
Yuri, what are you doing we want to
leave, not stay.

                    YURI
It misunderstood, it thought I wanted
to leave shuttle not ship.

          *(SAL is walking up the walkway
          and is holding the bomb in her
          hand, the timer reads 30
          seconds to detonation. Her
          face is badly injured from the
          laser cutter and she looks
          mad.)*

                    SAL
Looks like we are all going to die!

                   DMITRY
Shoot her Yuri!

          *(Yuri takes out his laser
          cutter and fires it at her
          face, she falls to the floor
          clutching the bomb.)*

                   DMITRY
Erm, stupid voice activated crap. We

just want to go to Earth, back home to
Russia!

> (The walkway retracts and the
> shuttle starts to vibrate
> making a low humming sound.
> The shuttle begins to move. It
> rises up above the other black
> ovoid shapes and shoots out of
> the shuttle bay at lightning
> speed and heads towards Earth.)

YURI

Dmitry, you did it. Quickly, let's get
in seats.

> (In the shuttle bay, SAL lies
> on the floor and the timer on
> the bomb reads one second.)

SAL

No!

> (The bomb explodes causing a
> chain reaction throughout the
> ship. One area then another
> ignite into a ball of fire.
> Yuri and Dmitry are holding
> tight to their seats inside
> their little shuttle, when a
> final huge explosion from the
> alien ship occurs, hurling
> objects and debris in all
> directions. They are about to
> crash into the surface of the
> Dome when just at the moment of

impact it disappears.)

                    DMITRY
We did it Yuri, we did it!

          (From the final explosion, a
          shock wave heads towards their
          shuttle and it begins to spin
          out of control.)

               SHUTTLE COMPUTER
Voice commands are now off line,
switching to manual control override.

          (A display console appears in
          front of them with various
          dials, displays, buttons, rods,
          wheels and levers. There seem
          to be hundreds to choose from.)

                     YURI
What's happening?   What do we do now?
The ship wants us to fly...

          (Dmitry grabs a lever and pulls
          it and they speed up.)

...Try something else...

          (The ship is now shaking
          violently and flames are
          leaping over the window.)

...We are on fire...

          (Dmitry pushes a square button

*with a fire extinguisher shape
on it and white powder covers
the outside of the window.)*

...The fire is out, but we are going
too fast Dmitry, we will burn up at
this rate, we won't survive the
descent. Press something!

DMITRY
I will try this.

*(Dmitry pushes a button that
looks like a car brake pedal
and they start to slow down.
The shuttle stops spinning and
continues towards Earth.)*

YURI
What about steering Dmitry?

DMITRY
I will try these arrows...

*(Dmitry pushes the left arrow
and the shuttle goes left.)*

...Looks like we are winning Yuri.

*(They descend through the
clouds, still going very fast.
The ground now seems to be
getting very close.)*

YURI
Press that brake pedal button again.

*(They slow down a little, but
then start to accelerate. The
ride becomes quite bumpy. They
now see the city of Moscow
beneath them.)*

DMITRY
Look! It is St. Basil's Cathedral and
Red Square. Look! It is clock tower -
7.40pm. It is good to know time of
death.

*(Yuri pushes and pulls on the
levers and buttons in front of
him like a mad scientist at
work.)*

YURI
We have nothing to lose now.

*(The shuttle starts to slow
down as they head towards the
city, then everything becomes
silent.)*

SHUTTLE COMPUTER
Prepare for emergency landing, and
please remain seated.

*(The controls disappear and the
seats move back from the
window. The shuttle levels out
and they hit the ground hard;
sliding along a road, before
crashing into the reception*

area of the Four Seasons hotel.
They come to a sudden stop in
front of two big doors.)

                    DMITRY
I don't know what you did, but it
worked.

        (The walkway extends out into
        the hotel reception area.)

                SHUTTLE COMPUTER
Emergency exit now available, please
disembark.

                    YURI
We did it Dmitry, we did it!

        (Yuri and Dmitry look at each
        other and smile.)

                    DMITRY
C'mon, let's get out of here.

        (Yuri and Dmitry walk out of
        the shuttle and stand in the
        reception area in front of the
        two big doors. The doors open
        and the Russian Prime Minister
        Kantcoughsky, is seen holding a
        piece of fish on a fork and is
        standing next to a waiter. He
        stares at Yuri and Dmitry, his
        mouth is open. Behind the
        Prime Minister is a big banquet
        with guests and a few members

of the Press.)

DMITRY
I hope we are not too late for banquet,
I do believe we are guests of honour.

(The Prime Minister drops his
fork along with the fish.)

YURI
Look Dmitry, they couldn't wait. They
are already on fish course.

DMITRY
Quick Yuri, check to see if card with
your signature is in stomach.

(They both laugh.)

YURI
Here comes the Press Dmitry...

(Some members of the Press walk
towards them. Yuri pulls out
his video camera and throws it
towards a Press
representative.)

...If you want a story, play this!

(A television hangs down from
the reception's ceiling of the
hotel and a reporter is
speaking.)

212

NEWS REPORTER

...In other news today... An electrical fire has broken out on the H.M.S Victorious and a 13 year old girl has beaten the world record for cucumber eating by swallowing 97 Persian cucumbers in under an hour...

To be continued...

Dmitry and Yuri celebrate their return home in:

DOWNFALL - PART I

If you enjoyed this book and would like to be notified of my next release, please subscribe to the *News, Events and Much more* section of my website under the 'Contact' heading. If you have time, please rate and leave a review on Amazon to help increase awareness of this series. Many Thanks, Sam Lucas.

To see the complete collection of books in this series, please go to: www.samlucasbooks.com